A soccer match between a scruffy bunch of undernourished Allied prisoners of war and the elite members of the German national team suddenly becomes an international confrontation.

MAJOR VON STEINER

The German propaganda officer who thinks up the idea as a morale-building activity only to find that it has become a propaganda tool for the Nazis.

CAPTAIN COLBY

A former English soccer star whose job it is to forge the Allied team into a unit that will match the strength of the Germans.....and maybe more.

HATCH

A brash American whose athletic prowess makes him a natural goalkeeper despite his unconventional style. For him, though, the result of the match is secondary to his greatest desire.....ESCAPE.

VICTORY

LORIMAR presents

A FREDDIE FIELDS PRODUCTION

A JOHN HUSTON FILM

SYLVESTER STALLONE

MICHAEL CAINE

MAX VON SYDOW

PELÉ

"VICTORY"

music by

BILL CONTI

screenplay by

EVAN JONES and YABO YABLONSKY

story by

YABO YABLONSKY and

DJORDJE MILICEVIC & JEFF MAGUIRE

directed by

JOHN HUSTON

produced by

FREDDIE FIELDS

A PARAMOUNT PICTURE

VICTORY

Yabo Yablonsky

Based on the screenplay by
Evan Jones and Yabo Yablonsky.
Story by Yabo Yablonsky and
Djordje Milicevic & Jeff Maguire.

BANTAM BOOKS
Toronto • New York • London • Sydney

VICTORY
A Bantam Book / August 1981

ISBN 0-553-20124-7

Published simultaneously in the United States and Canada

Bantam Books are published by Bantam Books, Inc. Its trademark, consisting of the words "Bantam Books" and the portrayal of a bantam, is Registered in U.S. Patent and Trademark Office and in other countries. Marca Registrada. Bantam Books, Inc., 666 Fifth Avenue, New York, New York 10103.

PRINTED IN THE UNITED STATES OF AMERICA

0 9 8 7 6 5 4 3 2 1

I would like to dedicate this book to the memory of my father. A guy who went through life armed only with a smile, a joke, and a cigar jammed into his mouth. He died rich because lots and lots of people loved him, and that's a lot to say about any man.

Carmel, California
December 1980

VICTORY

CHAPTER ONE

Colby stared at the white light that beamed from the guard tower and felt its way through the officer's hut. It was exactly 1:37 in the morning and every officer in the "oflag" knew that Freddy Williams was somewhere out in the yard pacing the moving beam in well rehearsed moves. In spite of the evening cold, sweat drenched Colby's body. He clenched his teeth against the rising gorge of anger and his sense of total futility. Of the dozens upon dozens of escape attempts, he knew of only two that had succeeded. The rest were failures and the men were either killed or rotting in solitary.

"The bloody, bleedin', bastard rulin' class. When will the fuckers stop this murderous honor game of theirs and stop sending boys out to be slaughtered or torn by dogs or impaled on the barbed wire. The bloody fuckers," he thought.

Hut three was the second stop in a plan that called for four quick dashes and drops. Freddie Williams half dragged, half crawled his way into the shadow of the hut's underbelly. His face was corked black and his eyes stared at the guard tower from beneath the folded brim of a black knit cap. Just as Freddy knew he would, the guard, who he had named "Stargazer," turned and looked to the heavens. The young man drew a breath and ran in a crouch six yards to a corrugated iron supply shack whose hinges he had previously greased and oiled. Its door opened noiselessly, and in an instant he was one with the shovels, picks, and hammers. The young man watched the throw of the powerful lamps until their beams met. This was his cue to go. He quickly crossed himself, closed his eyes for a fearful instant, then flung himself to the ground. Freddy crawled the last stretch crab-like to the first strand of wire, rolled over onto his back, and whimpered as the salt of sweat flowed from his sopping brow and stung into his eyes.

"Oh God," his mind screamed, "oh, my good God!"

He fumbled for the wire cutters and clipped the first strand. The sound of the popping wire was thunderous, as was the beat of his heart and the rasp of his breath. He wormed forward to the clean barbless wire that carried enough electrical current to kill, raised and propped it with a foot-and-a-half length of broom handle, and waddled towards the center section, which was a mad maze of rolled barbs. Working from the top down, he began to cut, and just as he had planned and dreamed, the wire began to fall away. Now all the fear was gone. It would be just a matter of minutes and he would be at his goal—the most vulnerable spot in the prison's security—the main gate. He unconsciously began to smile, his breathing eased, he was about to roll onto his stomach when the "stargazer" spotted him.

"Halt!" the guard called. "Halt!" And sirens began to wail.

Colby's heart chilled at the first call to halt and he shouted something that was lost in the scream of the alarm. The searching lights flicked through the hut and the prisoners bolted from their beds and stumbled to the windows to try to catch a glimpse of Williams.

Armed men with dogs appeared on the double and a voice was heard shouting, "*Aufstehen!* Get up, Englander. . . . *Aufstehen!*"

In a gesture that said, "I am unarmed, I surrender," Freddy rose slowly, lifting his arms away from his sides and to the heavens. "Stargazer," a 45-year-old recruit with only six months in uniform, nervously touched the trigger of his machine gun, and the boy tossed forward onto the wires, blood spurting from his lips, blood glistening silver as it dripped onto the black of his camouflaged sweater.

"The fuckers," Colby shouted. "The dirty murdering fuckers."

A Mercedes staff car followed by a vintage Citroen flying a Red Cross flag moved through the jungle of pine. It was early morning, and although the sun had topped the trees, there was still the chill of night in the air. Major Kurt Von Steiner smiled benignly at Herr Becker, the pink Swiss gentleman with whom he shared the glove-leather rear seat of the car. Von Steiner's mind was still reliving his last days in Russia, the white endless reaches of snow, the mud and the dead. His three years in combat had not prepared him for the job his wounds had earned him at the propaganda ministry, and he was bored and annoyed at the rolling r's of Becker's Switzerdeutsch.

Kurt's eyes moved away from the Swiss and stared beyond the head of the driver. A bevy of pheasant pecked along the side of the road, and at the auto's approach, they took to the air with a flurry of panicked wings. For a while, as if he were guiding the car, a large male flew before the windshield, then eased to the left and disappeared into the black forest.

Although the men at the gate expected the Red Cross delegation, it was a full ten minutes before the automobiles were admitted into the prison. The Mercedes moved through the gates with a growl of low gear and bucked under the nervous clutching of the driver. It crossed the triple strands of barbed wire and stopped within the compound. The Swiss' eyes were wide and alert: this routine trip had suddenly turned up a surprise. Never before had he been greeted by guns, by people with such intent looks.

Over the barking of the dogs and the hysterical shouts of the guard, Von Steiner could clearly hear the chanting of hate.

"Bastards!!! Murderers!!! Killers!!! Scum!!!"

A voice rose above all the others. It was high pitched, almost feminine.

"Bastards . . . fucking Hun killers!" Then the voice broke. It sobbed, "Fucking Huns . . . fucking killers . . ." and the Major broke into a sweat, his hands shaking uncontrollably. He knew their voices, saw their faces. It had been less than a year since he was one of them. He saw in his mind the endless lines of thousands shivering in the Ukranian cold. Disarmed, dishonored, hungry. He stared down at his trembling hands, studied them, then he felt the onrush of tears and quickly left the auto.

Captain Sherlock peered through the window of Colonel Waldron's quarters. With his bifocals slipped to the edge of his nose, he looked more the college don than the leader of a band of commandos that had demolished almost as much German rolling stock as any deep penetration raid by the RAF. He rested his head in his open palms and chewed nervously on the inner edge of his lips, then he turned into the small room.

"They're coming, sir."

Waldron looked to Major Phillip Rose, his intelligence officer, and there was a trace of irritation in his expression. He did not particularly like the idea of meeting the Swiss, whom he regarded as profiteering and more German than the Germans.

"Phillip, may I have the depositions of the death of young Williams."

"Of course, sir."

He immediately produced the file, a stack of handwritten papers tied by a string. Waldron took them in hand and walked to the window where he studied the approach of the camp Kommandant and the Red Cross investigators.

"A chummy looking bunch, aren't they, Rose?" Waldron said. "All drunk on the heady wine of good conscience. The bastards even look alike."

Rose sensed the colonel's irritation and avoided his eyes by closely focusing on the approaching men.

"But we do need them, sir. Without them there would be no protest at all, and the goons would have a completely free hand."

Waldron answered with a nod and grunt, then turned back into the room. He pulled the front of his white knit cardigan straight, started for the door, and the officer fell into step behind him.

Cedric Waldron was, as they say, born into the military. His grandfather, a captain in the 60th Royal Rifle Corps during the Sepoy Mutiny, had distinguished himself and had risen to colonel in a few short years. A feat, in those days, even in war, that suggested "brains and bravery"—a slogan that became a thing of family pride and obsession. His father, attending Addiscombe and Woolwich, was commissioned in the Royal Artillery, distinguished himself at the Battle of Marne, and was killed at Verdun. Cedric too attended Addiscombe, but soon, at the request of a family friend, Brigadier Wentworth, transferred to Sandhurst where he graduated third in his class. He was trained in cavalry, became something of an expert on the power of air, and then, again on request of the Brigadier, was sent to Black Africa as a military attaché to the consulate at Nairobi. His charm, his good looks, his uncanny ability with language, and, of course, his breeding led him from embassy to embassy and from higher rank to higher rank.

"This is a good war," he thought; "if it lasts

two years, I'll be a general." He saw his future clearly. When Paris fell, he was one of the last to leave. Captured on the road to Dunkerque without ever having fired a shot in anger, Colonel Cedric Waldron became a prisoner of war and his first command was as Senior British Officer at Gensdorf.

Camp Kommandant Willinger was all smiles, salutes, and handshakes; and although his breath smelled of brandy, he was as sober as Waldron and Rose had ever seen him.

"He's worried," thought Rose. "This afternoon's commotion has unnerved him."

The Kommandant continued with formal bows and clicks of the heels. "Colonel Waldron, you know Herr Becker, the Red Cross representative?"

"Of course, Kommandant. How are you, sir?"

"I'm well, Colonel. I hope we can clarify this ugly incident."

"I hope so, sir."

"And of course my aide, Oberstleutnant Strauss?"

Waldron nodded.

"And this is Major Von Steiner, from Berlin."

"Major."

"A pleasure, Colonel."

The brandy and what he perceived as good feelings took hold of the Kommandant, and he tried for humor.

"Colonel Waldron is, as you know, gentlemen, Senior British Officer, and this is Captain Rose, head of their escape committee." He giggled in self-amusement. *"Nicht wahr?"*

The men laughed politely, but Waldron saw no humor in it. He cleared his throat and turned hard eyes to the Swiss gentleman.

"Shall we move on to the site of the murder, Herr Becker?"

The Kommandant sobered immediately. "There was no murder here, Colonel. Your man tried to escape, he was challenged, he refused to obey a lawful command and was shot." He puffed his chest and his tone became indignant. "Although this is not a vacation resort. I try to run it entirely in the spirit of the Geneva Convention."

Becker tried for pacification with open palms and a bright smile that he flashed professionally from officer to officer.

"Of course, of course you do, Kommandant Willinger. Of all the camps I've investigated, yours rates among the finest."

Willinger's anger disappeared and he returned the Swiss' smile.

"You shall see, you shall see."

The men moved outside. With a strong stride, Waldron walked towards the southern perimeter of the camp. Becker moved to his side and the colonel took this opportunity to speak quickly to the investigator.

"Our Red Cross parcels have been delayed recently. We desperately count on them, you know."

"It is the bombings, Colonel. They have been very heavy."

"How is the war going?"

"It is turning slowly, but it is turning. Rommel's Afrika Korps is retreating and there is talk of invasion."

Oberstleutnant Strauss walked quickly to them. He had been ordered to stay as close as possible, to overhear as much as possible. When he saw the ordinarily stiff British colonel smile, he regretted the seconds it took to get to them.

The sound of a whistle stopped Von Steiner. He turned and focused across many strands of wire at a group of ragged men kicking a soccer ball across a flinty hard rock field. They were grotesque yet played a hard, mean game in their beaten combat boots and torn trousers. Major Rose paused beside him and pretended that he too watched the play. Rose was sure the man was not a regular army officer. Most of the military men walked through the compound with an attitude of superiority that could be discerned in their stride, in the arrogant turn of the head. This man was different, perhaps even more dangerous, and suddenly Rose felt the fear of recognition. He knew this man, but from where? When? Von Steiner turned suddenly and caught the man staring. He was silent for a moment, his gray-blue eyes sad, then he smiled.

"I was a footballer, you know."

"Oh?"

"Oh, yes. For many years." He fell silent again, then absently said, "Who is the tall man acting as referee?"

Rose followed his gaze. "Colby. His name is Captain John Colby. He's a flyer."

"Thank you," the German said in almost a whisper. Then he turned and walked towards the double stranded electrical gate that led to the recreation area. Rose noticed a slight limp, a dragging of his left boot, and his computer mind reeled, searching for the man that would fit the face and name.

"This man is dangerous," Rose thought. He knew it, he sensed it.

A heavy-set redhead dribbled the ball forward. He was clumsy but had the control and determination that came with years of playing in the back slum lots of Belfast. He turned, pausing for a pass, when a long-haired man leaped to his shoulders and brought him to the ground. In an instant, John Colby was across the field blowing his whistle furiously. In that same instant the redhead bolted to his feet with fists clenched.

"Bloody damn Yank," he sputtered. "What the bloody fucking hell do you think this is?" He could barely contain his anger. "Bloody fucking Yank!"

Bobby Hatch, like a beauty queen sprawled on a beach, propped his head against his hand and stared innocently up at the raging man. His eyes were large and brown, and there was humor in them when he spoke.

"What did I do?" he asked in New Yorkese. "C'mon, you guys, what did I do?"

The redhead would have none of it. "Get up, you bloody fucking bugger, and I'll rip your bleedin' head off."

Colby moved between the men.

"All right, McFarlin," he said, "I'll handle it." He glared down at the American. "God damn you, Hatch."

"What did I do?"

"You know bloody well."

"I was just goin' for the ball."

"You can't tackle like that in soccer. I've been telling you that for a year."

"You play English, I play American."

Colby clenched his fists and placed them on his hips. He looked down at the smiling face and there was a hardness in his voice.

"You try that bloody barbaric American style just once more,and you'll never play on this pitch again. Do you understand that, Hatch?"

Bobby got to his feet and brushed the dust from his torn fatigues. "What is this—a game for old ladies and fairies? You guys just ain't normal. That's your problem. You ain't normal."

Colby hefted the ball, tossed it into play, and Hatch was again into the thick of it. He knew the game well enough: he had been a prisoner for nearly three years, and only two things kept him sane. Soccer and the dream of escape. Bobby had been over the wall four times and had once made it as far as Stuttgart. Before the war, as a half-back for the University of Minnesota, he had almost been chosen all-American, and it was his superb condition as a trained athlete that allowed him to suffer the deprivations of solitary confinement, rise out of the darkness, return to the football pitch, play hard until his wind was up, and then run for the wall again.

John Colby entered the game. He came down the field with the grace and skill of a professional. The ball was his to do with as he damn well pleased, and there was no one skilled enough to stop him. He made it dance, he made it fly, he made it curve and run true. Hatch chased behind him, whooping like a crazed Indian, his arms fluttering wildly. In spite of himself, John laughed and intentionally footed the ball to the big American. Hatch caught it up, kicked for a goal and missed. The ball ran loose and Bobby dashed after it until it was stopped by the black boot of the gaunt Wehrmacht Major. The men's eyes locked for a moment, then Hatch smiled his idiot smile.

"Please, sir, can we have our ball back?"

Von Steiner, with a neat sidefooter, kicked the ball onto the field where Colby chested it to McFarlin.

"Thanks, Major," Hatch said and with a wave of the hand was back on the field. Kurt watched the game until Colby blew it to a stop.

"All right, officers and gentlemen, that's enough for today."

The men brushed the sweat and grime from their faces, and when Hatch kicked one of them lightly in the behind and ran, the entire team took after him in mock fury. John Colby laughed and started after them. He nodded at the gaunt German and was about to pass when the man stopped him.

"You are the sportsfuhrer here?"

Colby's reaction to Von Steiner was completely at odds with that of the intelligence officer, Rose. He found him so nonthreatening, so gentled that the Welsh flyer felt a sudden sympathy well up within him.

"No," he replied, "just one of the boys."

"Your name is Colby?"

John was surprised but disguised it with a smile.

"Yes."

Kurt looked into his eyes and studied them for a moment. "Colby? That is very familiar."

"It's a very familiar name."

There was a long pause before Von Steiner spoke again.

"Your men are very enthusiastic."

John laughed. "No bloody good, but enthusiastic."

"You play matches?"

John shrugged. "We've got a league. Four divisions. We even play internationals."

The German was impressed. "Ja, internationals? Is that so?"

"Well," said Colby through his grin, "as international as you can bloody well get in a prison camp. England, Ireland, Wales, and Scotland."

Von Steiner answered his grin with a small one of his own. "You call that international? It would be international if you played against Germany."

Colby slipped his hands into his pockets. Now it was his turn to hold the man's eyes, and he deliberately made his voice sound dominating.

"We'd murder you."

Kurt was amused. He liked the man's confidence and was about to say so when the Welshman's face suddenly came into focus.

"Colby!" he said, and his voice had a trace of surprise in it. "John Colby, Westham United, and England."

John cocked his head, and in spite of himself he was flattered and delighted. "That's right."

"You were sensational. Sensational," he repeated. "It's a shame the war has ended your career."

"Shall we say interrupted, Major?"

"Yes," Kurt said, "by all means let us say interrupted. It would be a pity if a talent like yours was destroyed by this madness we are engaged in. Yes, let us say interrupted."

The men stood in silence, then the Major

snapped a salute. "*Auf weidersehen,* Captain Colby."

"*Auf weidersehen,* Major."

Von Steiner turned and limped to the wires where the guards pulled themselves up straight and opened the gate to the warrior.

CHAPTER TWO

Waldron's thin fingers pointed at the swirl of barbed wire that had been cut in three different places.

"He was killed there, between the fences. As you can see, Herr Becker,"—he pointed to the large lamps placed on the guard tower almost directly above them—"when the guards found him, he knew he hadn't a chance. He raised his arms, surrendered, and was instantly gunned down."

Willinger protested. "The guards said he was climbing."

Waldron was outraged. "With his hands above his head, Kommandant?" He whirled and thrust the sheaf of tied papers into the surprised hands of the Red Cross representative. "These are the sworn depositions of eye witnesses."

"I too, have depositions, Colonel."

Waldron countered, his contempt festering each word. "I'm sure you do, sir!"

Becker quickly stepped between the officers, trying to hold them at bay with his engaging, infuriating smile.

"I will read all the depositions this evening, Kommandant, and both you and the colonel will have an answer in the morning. Is that satisfactory, gentlemen?"

Waldron drew a deep breath for a heated reply then thought better of it. He threw a quick formal salute to the Swiss and Germans and stalked back through the maze of wire to the officers' section of the prison.

The late winter was surprisingly mild, yet it was cold enough so that they could not open a window or do without the small fire that struggled within the black iron stove. As a result, the hut was a close and irritating place for the eight officers who lived in it.

Rose tucked his playing cards together then fanned them open for another look. It was another unplayable hand and he fought the impulse to toss his cards in and call it a night. The last months had been hellish for Rose. He knew it was a phase of prison life that all prisoners had to live through, but the irritation he felt was at the point of explosion. His bridge partner, Captain Sherlock, had bid an impossible two hearts. It took every bit of control for Rose to ride out the wave of anger that inundated him. The room suddenly felt close. It smelled, it was thick with smoke, and he wanted a drink. He wanted a woman, he wanted to escape, to be free.

Captain Robert Edwards, who had been a stock broker before accepting an artillery commission, spoke without lifting his eyes from his cards.

"The colonel's protest will be a waste of breath, I'm afraid."

Sherlock felt argumentative, but he kept control of his tone. "If we don't kick up a stink, Edwards, we give the bastards permission to do it again."

Edwards answered, "No bid."

Rose tapped his cards on the table top and looked across the room where Colby, with legs propped comfortably on top of the warm stove, was reading a tattered copy of the *Reader's Digest.*

"Colby, what were you talking to Jerry about?" Rose called.

John casually turned a page. He had been living with these men long enough to know their eccentricities, their highs and lows, and he immediately recognized the biting edge Rose's question carried. Sherlock heard it too, and he nervously cleared his throat in an attempt to catch Rose's eye and fend off the possible explosion. But Rose would not take the cue.

"Did you hear what I said, Colby?"

"It's none of your business."

Rose slammed his cards down. "Damn it, it is our business. You were seen in conversation with the enemy."

Colby looked away from the magazine and smiled at the men. "Listen to this," he said, waving the magazine. "It's a joke going around Berlin." He paused for effect. "If Hitler, Goering, and

Dr. Goebbels went down in an airplane, who would be saved?"

The officers looked dumbly at the blond Welshman.

"Who?" Hatch asked.

"The world," Rose snapped. "I read that six months ago. It seemed funny then, but not now."

Sherlock felt tension filling the hut. He knew Rose was going to press the Von Steiner question and decided to do it himself in a gentler, easier manner.

"What did he want, John? It's a legitimate question, you know. Phillip here *is* our intelligence officer."

Colby eased his feet off the stove onto the floor. "He recognized me."

Sherlock seemed pleased. "So the major is a football fan."

"More than that," Rose said eagerly, and all eyes turned to the intelligence major. "He's 'Dancer Steiner.' Remember him? He was part of Jimmy Hogan's 'Vunderteam' in '38 and played for Germany in '39. Now, what did he say to you, Colby?"

John pursed his lips and threw Rose a kiss. "He asked about invasion plans, Major, and I told him I would speak but only under torture." He was angry now, and he hated the anger because he somehow felt that the Oxford educated Phillip Rose was baiting him, and he was taking it hook, line, and sinker. "Now what the hell difference could it make what I said? What do I know that would be of any use to him or anyone else for that matter? I'm not involved in any of your idiotic escape plots. All I know is that a pack of cigarettes will buy two eggs and that a tin of Red

Cross beef will buy a pack of cigarettes. What else is there to know in this Godforsaken hole?"

He suddenly realized he was standing over the little man, that his hands were tensed, that he was about to hit him. He drew a deep breath and exhaled loudly. "Wow!" he said. "Wow, I'm sorry, Rose, I'm truly sorry. You have your escape committee and I have my football pitch. We're both trying for the same damn thing and that's keeping sane until this fucking war is over. I'm sorry." He extended his hand and it was a moment before the major took it.

Bobby Hatch crawled the length of a newly dug drainage ditch. It was an infantry crawl—elbows bent as if to cradle a rifle, butt low, knees and toes digging, then thrusting forward. He paused at the sound of a nearby vehicle starting up, waited until the driver slipped it into gear, then rose and ran a short distance to a shadowed place between huts. He drew a deep breath, tucked his arms and rolled until he was completely engulfed by the dark underside of the building. Hatch had been there before, three times within the week and twice the week before. The new drainage ditch made his run easier, and when he assumed his watching position, he was quite comfortable, almost at home in the darkness. He drew out a stub of a pencil and began jotting down on the back of an envelope every step and turn the distant sentry took as he made his rounds. Time and again the man performed perfectly. Thirty-three steps, a pause at the wires, then a turn. He watched and counted, watched and counted until his head nodded to his chest.

In late September, southern Ontario exploded in color. The lake, like a huge black mirror set in a frame of flaming fall leaves, reflected billowing white clouds. The sound of the speedboat brought Bobby to his feet. He walked to the far edge of the porch and watched it as it cleaved through the water. It was the right place in the world for him to be at this moment and Hatch felt himself relaxing. He had just received his lieutenant's commission in the Canadian Army and knew that once this weekend was over and he returned to his outfit, it was just a matter of time before he was shipped. The past eight months had been an emotional nightmare for Hatch. His mother had died a week before his graduation from the University of Minnesota, his dream of being chosen all-American had not materialized, his closest friend, Bill Hadley, who had volunteered for the RAF, had been killed over London. The world was at war and being an engineer seemed futile and stupid. He slipped out of his cardigan, leapt the porch's rail, and ran down to the pier to greet the speedboat.

Pamela Thompson and her sister, Carrie, were as rich and as spoiled as seven million dollars could possibly make them. They also had charm, laughed easily, and Bobby Hatch adored them. They knew that this weekend would be the last for a long while and they were going to do everything possible to make it great.

He helped the girls out of the boat, hefted the box of groceries and liquor to his shoulder, and the three ran laughing the length of the pier towards the house.

Carrie pushed the loaded cart into the bedroom. It was stacked high with an assortment of sand-

wiches, fruits, liquor, glasses, and two containers of ice. She wore a French maid's apron and cap and was gloriously blond and naked beneath them. The girl carefully measured three drinks and turned to the bed where her sister, impaled by Bobby Hatch, made small noises which counterpointed her slow grinding movements.

A shouted command sent a jolt of adrenalin through his body. How long had he been asleep? An hour? Two? Hatch looked down at his hands. They still clutched the envelope and pencil stub but were trembling uncontrollably. His lips moved as he mouthed silent words. "You dumb fuck, don't ever, ever fall asleep again, do you hear? Ever!"

Kommandant Willinger stepped out of a hut that Bobby had checked off as deserted. The German was laughing, and the woman under his arm sang a slurred tune that Bobby, in his terror, thought to be "Chattanooga Choo-Choo." The guard signalled and a staff car that had been parked on the dark end of the barracks pulled out and eased to a stop before the Kommandant and his lady. A tall SS driver leapt out and opened the rear door. Another black-suited soldier sat at attention on the front seat.

"My God!" Hatch gulped. "They could have moved a fuckin' army in on me and I wouldn't have known it." The words repeated in his mind. "A fuckin' army!"

It took a full ten minutes for him to control his nausea. He waited for the car to leave and the sentry to resume his pacing, then he rolled out into the light and ran in a crouch towards the shelter of his hut.

Like a blond gnome, Colby sat on a football and stared out across the pitch watching the men stumble, fumble, and fall. The game was a comedy of errors, and Bobby Hatch was top banana, chief of clowns. The American played goalie with a practiced nonchalance. Every save he made looked accidental. He would fall on a ball or let his legs slip out from under himself as he blocked a straight and strong kick that would have scored. Hatch always got to his feet with an amazed look and a self-deprecating joke. Now he paced before the goal, shouting to the players.

"Hey, let's go, let's go! Let's see the damn ball!" He clapped his hands together. "Let's go, babies. Let's play ball!"

There was no doubt in Colby's mind that Robert Hatch was a natural athlete and an intelligent man who, for his own reasons, chose the guise of a fool. He liked the American, and he knew they were friends in their own particular ways.

Von Steiner passed the check point and limped towards Colby, who caught sight of him out of the corner of his eye and got to his feet.

"Hello, Major."

"Captain Colby."

It was a moment when they almost shook hands, but Hatch called from across the pitch.

"Hey, Dancer, whaddyasay, baby?"

The Major laughed. "Dancer. I haven't heard that name in years. Was it you who recognized me, Captain?"

"Yes," Colby lied, "it was. I saw you play for Hogan."

The German lowered his eyes as pictures of friends and fragments of fragile moments flashed through his mind. He began a slow walk along the touchline and Colby followed.

"What's the verdict on Williams?"

Von Steiner shrugged. "A regrettable mistake. What else could they call it?"

John kicked at a loose stone and it rolled between the wires some six yards from the pitch.

"The whole bloody war is a regrettable mistake."

"I agree."

"Do you?" There was a cold, cynical edge to Colby's voice.

The major stopped and turned his sad eyes to the Welshman. "You can believe me or not, it is nothing to me, but all wars are a mistake. We have both been to the great event, and we both know the truth of it. Wouldn't it be a challenge, Captain, if nations could settle their differences on a football pitch?"

Hatch made one of his spectacular saves at the goal, and both men turned to the sound of the team's jeering.

John laughed and pointed to the pitch. "How about them as front line troops? I can see the headlines now. 'Colby's Commandos win another for old John Bull.' " He laughed again.

"It's not the worst of ideas, Captain Colby." Von Steiner unconsciously pulled at the stiff neck of his tunic. "How would you like to play a match against a team from the Wehrmacht? A team from the army base nearby?"

John still had a smile on his face when he asked, "What for? To settle the war?"

"Unfortunately, no. Let us say for morale."

"Yours or mine?"

"Both. I am bored, very bored, and this camp

could not be the most stimulating place in the world for you, either." He paused, allowing the words to settle in. "Is it, Captain?"

"What sort of a team?" Colby asked, choosing to ignore the major's barbed question. He dug the toe of his boot into the thick-grained sand. "Are they any good?"

"I haven't chosen a team. At the moment it is just an idea."

"It's not an order? You can't make us play."

"No," Kurt said emphatically. "No, it is a challenge."

Colby's heart began to pound. The excitement of a game, a real game, was almost more than he could endure. He felt his face flush, and it took all of his small town Welsh cunning to suppress a show of naked glee.

"No," he said, and thrust his hands into his pockets. "No chance. It would be a washout, a complete disaster."

"Why?"

"Why? For crying out loud, man, look at them."

The major's eyes glanced to the field. They did look pitiful, and Colby pushed the point home. "They're bloody hopeless in those clothes. And look at them, those flaming great boots make 'em look more like a herd of elephants than players." He shook his head. "No, they can't play football. Those bleeders can hardly stand up."

Von Steiner shrugged. "Boots are no problem, Captain. They can be supplied."

"Boots!" John said, his voice dripping with contempt. "How about gear? Basic gear, proper shirts and shorts? They've got to look like a team and feel like men before I'd let them onto a pitch."

"I . . . I don't know if I can do that," Von Steiner said and shrugged helplessly. "I'm sorry. Truly."

He turned and was about to step away when Colby, in a panic, reached out and touched his shoulder. Never in his life had he wanted anything more than this game—never.

"Major," he said, and the German turned to him. "I want to play, and I know you do too. So let's put all our cards on the table. You don't have to be a professional to see that my men are in no condition to play against a team. They'd be chucking their guts up in the first five minutes of a real game." He spoke so quickly that it took seconds for him to regain his breath.

Von Steiner felt the man's anxieties and knew he was correct about everything. He too desperately wanted a game, and he acknowledged that the men he saw gasping up and down the pitch were truly in no condition to play.

"What would you need?"

"Everything," John said, and when Von Steiner stood his ground waiting for him to continue, he knew he had him. "Special rations, eggs, meat, fresh vegetables." He paused, then dared, "And beer. A good team should smile once in a while."

The sad-faced major laughed. "Anything else?"

"Yes, if there's to be a team, I'd like us to billet together. Our own barracks, our own area, and it can't be just officers. I'd like a pick of the lads from the stalag. Can you do that, Major?"

"I don't know, Captain, but I will try. I will surely try."

Above them a V-shaped formation of geese winged north. Gleeful conversation honked between them, and both men stared silently at the sky, awed and respectful of creatures who had the freedom of the heavens.

CHAPTER THREE

In the care of two middle-aged guards, forty enlisted men marched towards an enclosure. It was a ragged line and no one, including the British NCOs, cared enough to try and bring the men into anything resembling a military formation. Anton, the younger of the two Germans, called the men to a halt, and his partner, Hans, began unlocking the gate that led into the wash house area.

Hatch leaned against a hut a short distance away and watched as Helmut stopped his rhythmic pacing and joined his friends with a loud greeting. Bobby lit a cigarette and passed it to McFarlin. The redhead drew on it and eased his head back onto the sun-warmed boards of the barracks.

"What do you see that I don't see? There's no way out of there."

Hatch nodded. "You can't disappear down the drain, that's for sure."

A British sergeant called a command and the men entered the wash room in groups of four. The three guards followed the last man in and closed the door behind them.

"You know those goons?" McFarlin asked.

"Yeah," Hatch said. "Helmut, Hans, and Anton. If vaudeville wasn't dead, they'd be a knockout comedy team. Hans has six kids, Helmut is the one who sells us the eggs, and Anton has the whistling chest." His eyes scanned the empty enclosure.

McFarlin offered him the cigarette.

"No thanks."

"What do you carry 'em around for then?"

His eyes read every inch of the area. "I don't know. It's an old trick I saw in a prison movie once. It makes you seem nonchalant, like you're thinking of broads and not going over the wall. I think I saw George Raft do it once. I don't know."

The men waited, staring at nothing. Hatch reached for a stone and threw it with some accuracy at a flock of black birds that dotted the wires. He missed and cursed quietly. The crows enjoyed the twirling strands of the fence. They congregated on the outer lines, mocked the men that were caged, and used the taut bars as trampolines. They would land, bounce, and in what seemed like fits of laughter, take to the air when the enraged prisoners threw stones and bits of debris in their direction. They were overfed, were never hit, they were free, and every man in the camp despised them. Bobby checked his watch, and there was a gleam in his eye when he looked back at the Irishman.

"McFarlin, me lad," he said, mocking the man's brogue, "do you see what I see?"

The man double-, then triple-checked. "No, Bobby, I don't see a thing."

That's the point," he said, grinning like a madman. "That's exactly the point." He pulled the butt from the redhead's hand and walked away whistling.

When pushed by necessity, Captain Donald Pyrie could come up with almost anything. Forged documents, visa stamps, worker or business men's clothes with a French or Swedish cut. With the aid of a former watchmaker, he developed a camera that, if the subject stood still long enough, took excellent photos. Because of Pyrie's extraordinary ability, he was an integral part of the committee's hierarchy and sat beside Waldron as the colonel considered the merits of this month's escape plans.

Pyrie shook his head to a plan submitted by three men who had been transferred into Gensdorf only four months before and were itching for a chance at the wall.

"I can get them the civilian sanitation uniforms, but we've tried that way before and Jerry seems obsessed with garbage. We never got through. They check their trash closer than they do their larders. If necessary, I can get enough eggs to bake a cake large enough for a decent coronation, but no way, gentlemen, can we get near their garbage." He looked to Sherlock and Rose, and both men smiled their agreement.

"He's right," Sherlock said, "the bloody Hun is obsessed with garbage."

"Then we're agreed," Waldron said. "Request denied. What's next on the agenda, Sherlock?"

"Colby's requested permission for a football match against the Germans."

"Whose idea?"

"That Major Von Steiner's. He's already pulled the strings necessary to outfit some of our boys."

Waldron leaned back in his chair and toyed with his baby smooth chin. "Seems there's a precedent for this, isn't there, Phillip?"

"Yes, sir. 1919, the Western Front. Our boys against the Jerries."

"Right. Yes, I recall now." He was slightly amused. "Seems they played all day and then came out and slaughtered each other the next." He turned to Sherlock. "Where is this to be?"

"Marburg."

"Phillip?"

The computer fed out. "Marburg. It's a small town about eighteen miles to the southeast. Twenty-five thousand population." He paused for a moment while fixing a picture of the town in his mind. "It'll be a small stadium. Main road north-south, railway line east-west."

Waldron looked about the table. "I have nothing against it in principle. What do you say, Sherlock? Anything to it?"

The scholarly looking commando thought for a moment then nodded his approval. "It's a chance to get eleven of us outside the wire. With any luck, one or two will stay there. I can't think of a negative."

Waldron brought it up for a vote. "Gentlemen?"

"No negative," said Rose.

"No negative," Pyrie echoed.

"Then we let him go," Waldron said with finality. "When is it to be?"

"The time hasn't been arranged yet, sir."

"Keep me informed. This could be interesting."

A sharp knock at the door turned them.

"Who is it?"

"Captain Hatch, sir."

"Just a minute, Captain," Rose said. He nervously tapped his pencil on the desk top. "That Hatch is up to something. He's been out of the hut every night for the past week. Whatever he has in mind, he's surely doing his homework."

"What else have we got, Sherlock?"

"One more, sir. Peter Bailey has a plan for pole-vaulting the south fence."

"Pole-vaulting the south fence!" Waldron said, shaking his head. "Pole-vaulting? My God, tell him he's refused, Sherlock, but say it gently. I think old Bailey is dropping off the deep end." Again he shook his head. "All right, let's have Hatch in."

Pyrie opened the door and Hatch walked directly to Waldron and saluted. He had approached the committee before and knew its formalities.

"So," said Waldron with a fatherly smile. "How is this one going?"

"Well, sir, the whole thing depends on the fact that some of the goons don't patrol when the men are having a shower."

"Some of them?" Rose asked sharply.

"Yes, like Hans and Anton."

"Do you know these guards?" Waldron asked Sherlock.

"Yes, sir. Third rate reservists."

Hatch nodded and continued quickly. He had the plan clearly formed in his head and he didn't want to lose his audience. He needed the committee to make it a reality. "At least one of them should be outside the wash house walking back and forth, but they know we're inside having a shower; so they come inside, lean against the door, have a smoke if they can bum one, and I think if somebody went missing they wouldn't report it."

Waldron looked doubtful, and Sherlock voiced his dissent. "Why not?"

Bobby sensed the group's disapproval and his defense poured out, words tumbling over words. "They wouldn't be sure. They'd think they'd miscounted. They'd leave it until roll call." Waldron held up his hand to stop the flow, but Bobby continued. "I could be gone for days before they found out."

"Slowly, slowly, Hatch. You're going too fast. I'm still not clear on how you're going to get out of the wash house," Waldron said, but his interest was piqued, and he nodded for Hatch to continue.

"Through the vent on the top of the shower room. It leads to a storeroom or something."

Rose involuntarily interrupted. "It was built as a lavatory to match the one on the German side."

Hatch's eyes widened slightly. He had been studying the wash room for weeks and didn't have that piece of information. He was impressed. "That's right," he said, "that's right. And if I could get in there with something to pick the lock . . ."

Waldron broke in. "You'd be back in the enclosure where you started."

"Right sir," Hatch added eagerly. "But there's

nobody there! I'm all alone. I could go over the roof, through the wire, and then drop into the German compound."

"But you'd be naked," the encyclopedia said.

"Yeah," Hatch said forlornly, "that's the problem."

Sherlock chuckled, but the idea intrigued him. He smelled its merit. "No offense, old man, but how are you going to get out of the German compound naked?"

"I've got five or six good ideas."

"That's what we're here for, Captain, good ideas. And as long as it doesn't include pole-vaulting, we're ready to listen."

The officers laughed. It was their private joke, but Hatch joined them. He had something going, and he wasn't about to lose it.

Colby was up before muster, checked out with the guards, and was at the pitch by the time the sun had touched the horizon. For the first time in perhaps the entire history of armies, every able-bodied man had volunteered for a job. The lure, of course, was fresh eggs, milk, beer, and a good chance of kicking their captors even if only on the playing field. In three days of tryouts, Colby had narrowed the field down to about fifty good men. Some he had known as professionals, some were talented amateurs, and some were just brutes that he wanted for a psychological show of muscle.

Clipboard in hand, Colby paced the touchline like a panther seeking a meal. He was hungry for a team that could win, and it seemed to be forming.

A lithe, dark corporal went for the ball. He

trapped it neatly and brought it forward, looking for a man to pass to. He eluded two tackles then laid the ball in the path of a charging teammate. John knew the man. He had played against him and knew him as a hard driving back. He blew the whistle and trotted out onto the field.

"Nice going, Hayes."

The man wiped the sweat from his brow. "Thanks, Colby—or should I say, sir?"

"No, Colby'll do. We're going to live too close and work too hard for any of that officer nonsense." He gently rapped his shoulder. "You're on the team, Arthur. Welcome aboard."

"Good to be aboard," the lean man said. "Its not quite like playing for Manchester, but it's better than not playing at all."

John jotted Hayes' name down as Hatch, his hair matted with the sweat and grime of the pitch, ran up to him.

"Hey, Colby, how's about me? As long as you're writing, why don't you put me down?"

John waved him away. "Get out there."

"Hey!" he protested.

"Go on, Hatch. Get out there and play. I've too much on my mind to deal with you now." The American hesitated. "Go on now."

"Up yours." Hatch glared and ran back into the thick of it.

From behind the double strands of wire that separated the officers' compound from the pitch, Waldron and Pyrie watched the selections.

"Why aren't there more officers out there, Pyrie?" Waldron asked.

"There were, sir, but Colby eliminated them."

"Eliminated them?" For a moment the colonel was speechless. "What in the world can the man possibly be thinking?"

Pyrie shook his head. "I suppose he wants to pick the best team possible."

"He's mad as a hatter." Waldron could feel the hair rising on the back of his head. He was genuinely angry. "I don't think he's getting the point at all. Tell him to come see me. And soon." He turned and stalked towards his hut.

It rained that night and in the morning the pitch was a bog and the sky gray and threatening. John had no idea of the presence of blacks in the camp and was taken by surprise when a contingent of West Indians attended the tryouts. They stood off to themselves, shy dark birds among their gaudier, laughing white brothers. Colby whistled and pointed three of them onto the field. Two were useless, but the third, Luis Fernandez, was a phenomenon. He moved through the field of attackers as if they were there for his amusement. He balanced the ball on his chest, and when two opponents flung themselves at him, he nimbly dropped the ball, caught it with a kick and, with some of the best dribbling Colby had ever seen, shot it through the totally inadequate defensive play of the goalie and scored. It was an incredible 75-yard run without any assistance. The ball was as much a part of him as his arms and legs and striking smile, and he worked it as if it were on invisible strings. The normally raucous men strung out along the touchline to watch in silence and utter amazement as Fernandez, again without assistance, brought the ball down the pitch.

When the opposing team attacked almost en masse, he rose incredibly above the ruck and headed the ball in for a goal.

Colby watched with slackened jaws as Sid Harmer, a striker whom Colby had already chosen as a key offensive man, ran to him shouting. "Lord, oh Lord. Did you see 'im? Did you see 'im, John?"

"Lord, oh Lord is right," Colby said. He started out across the pitch and the striker followed.

"What's your name, man?"

"Fernandez," the soldier answered. "Luis Fernandez."

"You're good, Fernandez, do you know that? You're god damn good."

The man flashed a smile. "Yes sir, I know."

"Where in the world did you learn to play like that?"

"In Trinidad, Captain," he said in the easy calypso cadenced speech of the islands. "In the streets, my friends, we played with oranges, so the big ball was easy when it came."

"Oranges!" Colby's brows were raised as he turned to Harmer. "He played with oranges!" He turned back to the West Indian. "Could you use some extra rations, Luis?"

"Will there be oranges, Captain?" Luis joked.

"Yes. Oranges if I have to steal them and a bloody pineapple if there's one left in Europe." He extended his hand and the black man took it. "You're on the team, Fernandez."

Hatch, who had been part of the defense that tried to stop the black cyclone, trotted casually up to the group.

"Hey," he said, "hey, man, that was great."

"Thank you," Luis said humbly.

"You betcha," Bobby replied with a warm smile. Then he turned to Colby.

"How's about me? Did you see me?"

"Yes, I saw you," John answered dryly.

"So?"

"So—what?"

Hatch was suddenly in a fury. "So you've got your head up your ass, that's what. You wouldn't know a footballer if he crept up on you and pulled you by the short hairs. Who the hell do you think you are, God or something?"

Just as Colby was about to reply, the threatening dark clouds parted and a blinding rain drenched the pitch.

CHAPTER FOUR

Waldron looked up from the skimpy file before him and slowly shook his head at the officer that stood before him.

"I'm sorry, Hitchcock, but we've studied your plan from top to bottom, and it is our opinion that it would be suicidal. There are too many complications, any one of which could bring Jerry down upon you and your group. In all probability they'll choose to interpret your tools as weapons and use them as an excuse to murder you." He pushed the file away from him in a final gesture of disapproval. "I'm sorry. Come up with something else and we'll be glad to consider it."

The crestfallen man saluted then moved to leave.

"Oh, Hitchcock," Sherlock's voice stopped him. "Would you ask Captain Colby to come in, please?"

John entered with the grime of the pitch still on his face and etched black under his fingernails. He was exhilarated by the day's choice of players and it showed in his eyes, in the swagger of his gait.

"You wanted to see me, gentlemen?"

Waldron forced a smile. He liked the size of this potential escape. In a strange way, he had adopted it as his own and resented the fact that Colby had been ignoring his authority; never once since their first conversation had he so much as asked Waldron his advice or offered up the names of those selected to "go."

"Ah, yes, Colby," he said. "Thank you for dropping by."

John took a cursory look around the table and immediately knew something was wrong.

"Good of you to have me in," he said, as if it were an invitation to afternoon tea and the colonel was about to ask, "One lump or two?"

Waldron signaled to Pyrie, who reached under the table and unstrapped a small packet of tattered maps.

"We've a present for you, John."

Colby had never been called "John" by any of them. It unnerved him and he looked at the stack of maps as if it were a jug of hemlock.

"I thought you might like to have these, compliments of our friends in the village," Waldron said. "The map of Marburg is from an old guide book, but it's reliable, I should hope."

Colby looked from the maps to the men and thought, "What the hell are these maniacs talking about?"

"There's a fast train to Cologne at 5:33 every Saturday," Pyrie said, "and I've got my man on the manufacture of enough tickets for the entire team. Of course, not all of you will make it, but," he shrugged, "who knows? Stranger things have happened."

Waldron was smiling now. He was caught in the forward motion of the plan, he was feeling better, he was feeling control.

"If you look under the map," he said, "you'll see that they've a sketch of the stadium. A lot of it was done through memory, of course, but I feel they've accurately covered most of the exits, and there's an excellent prospective of the changing rooms. . . ."

Colby was incredulous. "Colonel Waldron, what in the world are you talking about?"

Waldron answered innocently. "I'm talking about your escape."

"My escape?" Colby practically stammered.

"Yes, of course," Sherlock grinned, projecting a great deal of self-satisfaction, "the whole team, if possible." He flicked a hand towards Pyrie. "Donald here has his team scrounging every bit of cloth they can lay their hands on." Then he became serious, almost officious. "You know, old man, you'll have to get them in for a fitting as soon as possible."

"One of the difficulties," Waldron added as a sting, "is that you've created this problem with the enlisted men." He cleared his throat. "They've a committee of their own, you know, Colby. And although we have communications with them, coordination won't be easy."

Pyrie spoke with a sudden touch of excitement in his ordinarily calm voice. "What about the lorry that takes them to the match? They can loosen the floorboards on the way in and drop out on the way back."

"It's possible," Rose conceded, but he didn't sound enthusiastic.

Colby looked incredulously from man to man. "Wait a minute. Just a bloody moment. What escape are you talking about? I'm not going to lead those men in an idiotic escape attempt. I'm putting a football team together."

Waldron backed off as if hit. "Are you mad, Captain?"

Sherlock rose to his feet, sputtering his indignation. "It . . . it's your duty as an officer, Colby."

"Duty my arse," the Welshman roared. "You're going to get a bunch of innocent men killed or tortured in those god damned solitary cells of theirs, and I won't be a party to it!"

"Certainly worth investigating, old boy," Rose said with remarkable calm.

"I'm not interested."

"Are you afraid?" Waldron said, and there was more than a bit of venom in his tone.

"Yes, I'm afraid," Colby shot back. "I'm afraid you've lost your fucking minds!" Anger made him breathless. "This escape thing of yours is an ugly bloody upper-class game, and not everyone is interested in playing it. Those blokes have done their job, and they just want to be left alone until this damned war is over." He stood silent, swaying slightly as if suddenly drugged. "Isn't it possible, just remotely possible, that some people think that way? I won't," he said softly, feeling the rage rushing through his body, "I won't lead them in an escape. They're going to play football, and if I can help it, they're going to win."

Waldron rose and met the captain's eyes. "That will be all, Colby. Thank you."

John turned, missed a step, then left the suddenly silent room.

CHAPTER FIVE

The light prismed through the crystal of the magnificent eighteenth-century chandelier and cast tiny rainbows onto the walls. The orchestra was military but was dressed for the occasion as formal civilians, black and white and starched, and glad to be playing Strauss. The dancers moved easily to their sound.

The huge buffet was stacked with cheeses, black Russian caviar, Greek dolmas, dumplings from Sardinia. It was a table set for victors.

Von Steiner flipped his lighter and lit the cigarette of Emma Von Boehmer, a dark-haired beauty who was General Lang's niece. Kurt was relieved that this act of being charming, if not out and out seductive, was not a duty but a great and unexpected pleasure. He liked her form, the total absence of Aryan loveliness. The wine made him reckless, and he was about to suggest his apartment above the Wilhelmstrasse, when Leutnant Mintz, Lang's aide-de-camp, moved to them, nodded his apology to the lady, whispered under the music, then hurried away.

"War," she quipped, then smiled, showing a slightly crooked tooth, an imperfection that made her even more attractive to the Major.

"Yes."

The smile vanished. "Come back for me, if you can."

"If I can."

Leutnant Mintz was a young man with a mission. His nervous eyes caught Kurt's, held for a split second reminder, then hypnotically focused at a point directly ahead.

"Your apartment is just across from the Swiss Embassy, is it not?" Emma asked.

"Yes."

In the soft, prismed light, her eyes were black. In the seconds of silence, the music seemed louder, the laughter around them sharpened by the wine.

"I don't know just when your uncle will release me, but I would consider it a privilege if you would accept my hospitality this evening." He gave the music a moment, then continued. "My valet, Corporal Kessler, will admit you."

"Do you have chocolate? I like chocolate."

It was the most erotic acquiescence Kurt had ever heard, and in the limousine that brought him across Berlin, he savored the word "chocolate" between his tongue and palate.

General Lang's instincts as a politician were much surer and much more committed to futures than those of any of his more courageous but less astute colleagues. There were hero soldiers who avoided him, knowing that he was dangerous and vain and would use his considerable power to hurt them if they somehow got in the way of his ambition.

Just after the assassination of Roehm, Lang, with his nose to the changing winds, embraced the party. And because he was a Junker, because his family was in steel and coal and it was still fashionable and socially correct for the elite to frown upon the Nazis, the general was accepted fully by Hitler and his clique. He had been to the front only once as part of an inspection team, yet his hand-tailored tunic was bejeweled with medals, and he had just been made military governor of a vast area that included Berlin.

Lang sat on a carved chair that was adorned with gold leaf eagles. He was seated behind a great black highly polished mahogany table. Beside him sat Carl Hoffman, a colonel who for a while served in the same regiment as Von Steiner and was one of the last to leave the Russian front. In the past, Hoffman had greeted Von Steiner with the warmth of a comrade who had seen the same guns and had faced a common enemy and danger. Now he was aloof and avoided the major's gray-blue eyes.

To Lang's right, a high-ranking party official sat slumped in a chair. His slouch showed his power and, in a sense, contempt for these men of the military. Kurt had never seen the man before, and no one thought to introduce him.

"How long have you been back from the front, Major?" Lang asked.

"Eight months, Herr General."

"And how long have you been with the Ministry of Propaganda?"

"Six months, sir."

"And this game was your idea?" He said the words slowly, and Kurt knew he was the mouse and Lang the cat and there was no way to avoid the game that was going to be played out. He glanced over at Hoffman, but there was no life in the man's eyes, no sign for him.

"Yes, sir, it was entirely my idea. I take full responsibility for it."

"Yes," said Lang, "I'm sure you do." The general's moustache rose, and Kurt thought he was possibly smiling. But he wasn't. "And you authorized equipment for the enemy?"

Von Steiner dared to correct him. "For the prisoners, sir. Yes, I did."

"And you informed no one of your actions? Not one of your superiors?"

"I did not consider it important, Herr General. Hardly worth anyone's notice."

This time Hoffman did react. His eyes shifted to the civilian, and Kurt was suddenly aware for whom this game was being staged. The wound in his leg suddenly began to hurt. He shifted his weight slightly, but remained rigid until the party man tapped the table with a silver pencil and drew all eyes to himself.

"Come, come, General Lang. Enough of this. I asked to meet Major Von Steiner not to reprimand him but to see the quality of the man. I am impressed. Initiative is what the party is based on. The ability to see into the future and act."

He gestured, and out of the shadow of the room Mintz appeared.

"A chair for the Major, Leutnant . . . Let me introduce myself," the party man said, "my name is Lorenz."

Von Steiner was uncomfortable in the high backed chair; for some reason his leg hurt more than it did when he was standing, but he managed a smile.

"A pleasure, Herr Lorenz."

"Thank you," Lorenz replied then turned to Hoffman and the General.

"War, as you know, Herr General, is like fashion, isn't it?" Lang nodded his agreement but hadn't the foggiest idea of what the man was getting at. "Change, change, change. Yesterday we were fresh and beautiful. Fortunes of war, you might say. But now we are beginning to look a bit ragged about the cuffs." He smiled, but there was no life in it, no mirth. "It seems to me that it is the job of the Propaganda Ministry to add a little lace here, a touch of silk there, and make it look new, fresh, victorious."

Lorenz reached for a wooden box that matched the mahogany of the table. Mintz quickly lifted the lid and the man drew a cigar. "Don't you agree, Herr General?" he pursued.

"Of course," Lang said slowly. "We will be victorious. We are the best in the world."

Lorenz placed the cigar between pursed lips, and Mintz leaned in, his lighter lit; but the Nazi maddeningly took his time lighting it. When he looked up, his eyes were hard. He focused directly at the general, and Lang felt fear.

"Yes, Herr General, we are the best. We are superior in everything. In power, in courage, in blood. But Rommel has been beaten in Africa, and the Allies, like ants, have climbed the mountains of Anzio and have a hold on a part of our continent."

He drew and blew a thick stream of smoke into the overheated atmosphere.

"The ants are everywhere. Some we can frighten, some we can destroy, some we can control—and we will control the course of this game." He turned his eyes to Kurt. "It will all be in your orders, Von Steiner. I like you, I like your imagination, and I know that I don't have to remind you that you are a soldier, and this is war."

A harsh wind blew off the Spree and whistled through the burnt and haunted walls of the old Reichstag. Kurt hoisted his collar and plunged his hands into the pockets of his greatcoat. Lorenz's words hammered through his head, hammered hard so that it hurt between his eyes. "What did he mean by, 'you are a soldier, and this is war?' Why was everything so twisted, so unclear?" All he wanted was to play football, to create an entity that would lessen the pain of this endless and bestial war. How insane Germany had become, how infectious the Nazi disease. Was no one immune? Pictures of the SS and how they killed in Russia ran nightmarishly through his brain. He saw the drawn Lugers, heard the shuffle of boots, the sound of bullets hitting the back of heads. His hands were suddenly moist, his fingers sticky as if they had been immersed in blood. He drew them out quickly, stared at them, then hurried along to the Wilhelmstrasse.

As Corporal Kessler opened the door, Kurt felt the instant warmth of the fireplace and was bathed in the almost tropical light of candelabras. Two crystal glasses stood beside a good Bordeaux that was uncorked and breathing. Mendelsohn's Scottish symphony, old and well used, scratched on the phonograph. He knew that Emma Von Boehmer had indeed come for her chocolate, and the colonel forgot his anger and smiled at the romantic corporal from Leipzig.

"Thank you, Kessler," he said, "that will be all for the evening."

Corporal Kessler, with a sly laughter in his eyes, replied, "My pleasure, Herr Colonel." He bowed and quickly walked to the kitchen.

Emma Von Boehmer was easily seduced. Her body was soft, smooth, almost perfect. She responded to Kurt's advances, but there was an emptiness to her lovemaking that Kurt could not fathom. There were moments when he could feel her passion rising, then for no discernible reason she became automatic, studied, even her groans seemed timed.

The lights of the candles flickered over her, he ran an open palm over the gold of her breasts, bent and gently kissed her. He was about to speak, when the sirens began. He touched her face, blew out the candles, and pulled the blackout curtain from the window.

Beams of strong lights pierced the sky, guns streaked insane patterns of criss-crossing tracers, brave men in machines fifteen, twenty thousand feet above the earth hunted each other, faced darkness and death, wet their flight suits, sat in excrement and sweat. He could see the guns flashing on the roof of the I.G. Farben building, felt the vibrations of their steady thumpthump. Then the Lancasters unloaded adding a new sound to the black song that men were dying to.

A bomber, caught in the web of light, struggled

to evade the streaking shells; then its engines flamed, adding a red flare to the crazy canvas of the black sky.

"Emma," he said, "come and see."

He turned to the girl and beckoned. "Emma . . ." he murmured and was struck by her form there in the light of the bomber's moon. She had slipped into his jackboots. Her knees were drawn, her legs spread, and her red-lacquered fingers, like graceful white-red serpents, danced over her vagina.

Kurt slipped into the bed and stared at her face, tense with pleasure and the force of her tightly shut eyes. Then her lips parted and a sound so deep, so passionate rose from so deeply within her that it reached out to him, entered his body, and, as if possessed, he began to tremble.

Hatch stood in a crowd of about fifty officers watching their mates playing volley ball. He cheered when they cheered, booed with them, and even laughed on cue, but his eyes were focused beyond the game into the wash house area. He pictured himself running across the open ground, counted the steps it would take, and computed the time of the run.

A lanky player jumped for a high and wildly hit ball, and Hatch, too abstracted to move, took the full impact of the player's body. He was sprawled on the ground, when Sherlock, helping him to his feet, gave him the news.

"You're on your way home, Hatch. The committee has considered your plan, and you've an appointment with the tailor and forger this afternoon."

Bobby leapt into the air and landed with a wide

grin spread across his face. "Terrific. God damn terrific." He threw his arm around the bespectacled man. "Fucking dynamite."

They walked a few steps in silence as Hatch began to absorb the reality of the news.

"The locksmith," he said suddenly, "I gotta see the locksmith."

Sherlock was amused. "Of course," he said, "but see the tailor first, that takes time."

They strolled across the yard chatting like old buddies. Hatch, in his enthusiasm, threw question after question at the man from the committee and only half-listened to the answers.

As if his nose had hit a wall of glass, Sherlock stopped suddenly, reeling back, and Bobby cursed quietly under his breath. "Well, I'll be a son of a bitch!"

Across the barbed wire, in what was now called the "player's compound," Colby, freshly groomed and in a newly pressed uniform, passed through the main gate and entered a Mercedes, the door of which was held by an SS man.

"Son of a bitch," Bobby murmured.

Colby leaned back into the soft leather of the rear seat of the automobile. It was three years since he had been out of Gensdorf. He stared out of the window, astounded at how large the world seemed.

The Mercedes entered a forest, passed through a small town, then turned onto the smooth black lanes of the autobahn. The naked winter trees were silhouetted against a sky that had turned gray and cloudless, and Colby was depressed.

The War Ministry was a dark granite monstrosity with Grecian pillars that supported an immense bas relief eagle topped by a circled swastika. Only the red and black banners that whipped in the bitter wind relieved the building's rigidity.

The black auto pulled to the high curb and was instantly approached by four soldiers. Two carried Mausers, one held a large overcoat. The fourth, a lieutenant, snapped a brisk salute. "Good afternoon, Captain Colby," he said in flawless English. "Welcome to Berlin."

John was speechless, and the lieutenant continued without a pause, ignoring his silence as he ignored the stiff and formal SS guards.

"I hope you enjoyed your trip?"

Colby found his voice. "Yes, yes I did."

"If you don't mind, Captain," he said, taking the overcoat from the soldier's extended arms, "I would appreciate it if you would slip into this." Then he became absolutely charming and spoke through a smile. "You do understand that the sight of a British flyer at the War Ministry would, at best, raise some eyebrows?"

John nodded again. "Yes, yes, of course."

He pulled the greatcoat over his shoulders and followed the young man's lead into the gaunt building.

An elevator attended by a statue-stiff sentinel opened for them. They entered, and without command, the operator closed the doors and the lift moved.

John felt the sweat of his anxieties form on his palms, soak his underarms, stain the back of his shirt.

The doors of the lift opened at the sixth level, and he was startled at the sight of the corridor he faced. It lacked any semblance of anything military. It had the lush, quiet, oaken feeling of the executive offices he hadn't seen in four or five years. The carpets muted the sound of their steps, and a smiling blond lady rose from behind a Louis Quinze desk and approached them with a subdued smile. Her uniform was smartly tailored, her hair coiffured. She said something in German to the lieutenant, who clicked his heels and ever so slightly bowed his head. Then she turned to the Welshman.

"You're expected, Captain. Would you please follow me."

She led Colby to a plush office and closed the door carefully behind him, leaving him alone. He suddenly became aware of the ridiculous long coat, unbuttoned quickly, flung it onto a chair, then walked to the center of the silent, empty office and turned slowly, examining the environment. There were pictures on the wall. Posed photos of athletes, action photos of players grimy and sweating, a portrait of an unsmiling Hitler, and between the leather-bound books on the black oak shelves were trophies, many trophies.

The sound of a closing door made him turn, and he looked into the gray-blue eyes of the smiling Wehrmacht major.

Von Steiner walked to Colby, his hand extended as if he were greeting an old friend. For some reason Colby could not fathom, the major's limp was more pronounced. There was pain in his eyes.

"Captain Colby, how are you?"

"I'm fine, Major, and you?"

"Fine, fine." He pointed to one of the leather chairs. "Sit, please." He hit a button on the intercom. "Kathlene, *zwei bier, bitte.*" Then he looked to Colby. "I thought you might like a beer."

"Yes, yes I would, thank you."

Colby stole another glance at the room. It began to stabilize. He was growing used to the idea of different spaces. He wriggled into the soft leather of the chair and looked at Kurt with a growing confidence. "What am I doing here?" he demanded. "Tell me, what the hell is this all about?"

CHAPTER SIX

Hauptmann Muller looked very much the way Colby remembered him when he played for the Italians in Milan. His hair was still cropped short, shoulders wide, waist trim. "Hoppy Muller" looked fit in his Wehrmacht uniform.

"You remember Captain Muller, don't you, Colby?"

"Of course," John said. He got to his feet and the men shook hands. "It's been a long time."

"Ja," Muller said, all the while sizing John up. "Another world, another age."

"Captain Muller is the coach of our National team. And a good one, I might add."

"Why not," Colby replied. "He was one of the best center halves I've ever seen on a pitch. Congratulations, at least you'll be sure of a job after the war."

"Thank you," Muller said, and the men sat.

It was polite and chummy, yet there was a tension that Colby could feel. He sipped his beer and decided that the ball was now with the Germans and that they would have to make the first move.

Von Steiner cleared his throat and fiddled with his cigarette lighter. "Our football match has been taken a little out of our hands."

"Oh?" said Colby.

"It has been decided that a German National team will play a combined team from the prisoners of war of the occupied territories." He flicked the lighter and lit a cigarette. "We will play on August 15th, in Paris."

"Paris?" Colby drew a deep breath. "That's crazy. I've got some good men, but no one good enough to take on a national team."

"Not so crazy," Kurt said and was suddenly on his feet. "Hauptmann here will assist me and make sure you have everything you need." He leaned forward and his voice dropped to an intimate tone. "Everything."

"What if I refuse?"

Kurt smiled and shook his head. "You won't."

He quickly walked to his side of the desk and pushed a dossier towards John.

"Look at these names. When I said occupied territories, I don't think you fully grasped the area I'm talking about." He sat on the edge of his desk watching Colby read down the list. "I'm sure you will recognize some of those names."

Until this moment, Colby had not realized the extent of the Nazi conquests. The list covered the entire continent. He looked up at Muller and Von Steiner in the gray uniforms of the Wehrmacht. They were truly the enemy, and he was a soldier, and the game, the innocent game that had been proposed, was now combat, deadly combat. He felt a surge of anger flash through him. "The bastards," he thought, "the rotten, bloody bastards. They want everything, everything." He wanted to slash out at the confident faces, but instead said quietly, "Yeah, there are some good players here." His eyes scanned the list. "British, French, Dutch . . . even Lofson. I almost forgot about the Norwegians."

He looked away from the file and fixed his gaze on the Wehrmacht major. "What about the Poles and Czechs? I mean, off the top of my head, I can think of about half a dozen East European players who would just have to be on that squad." He turned to the Captain. "Wouldn't you say so, Muller?"

"I suppose so," Muller said, but Kurt broke in immediately.

"That is impossible. I'm afraid I cannot let you have any Eastern Europeans."

"Why not?"

"It is impossible. I've been given orders to that effect directly from my commander. Officially they do not exist."

"Maybe not officially," Colby said, "but they do exist as players." He looked blankly at the officers. "Don't they?"

Von Steiner nervously drummed on the top of the desk. It was as if he played a silent, invisible piano that dominated all of his thoughts. John sensed an advantage and plunged for it.

"I don't know whether these Eastern European players are alive or dead, but you can find that out. I mean, as an officer and a gentleman you are obliged to give me a marginal chance of winning."

A squadron of Messerschmitts roared somewhere off in the distance, and for a long moment the sound of the fighters blotted out all sounds in the room.

"All right, Captain, make your list. I will see what can be done."

Colby reached for his tankard. He got to his feet and saluted the soldiers.

"To Paris," he toasted.

"To Paris," they echoed.

CHAPTER SEVEN

British enlisted men, under the supervision of German civilians, were everywhere. Some hammered siding, some cut and placed support beams; and as a result of this feverish activity, the new hut in the player's compound was entering its final stage of completion.

Colby left the players on the field and walked towards the construction. Although the uniforms Von Steiner promised had not yet arrived, the boots had, and their effect on the team was astounding. For the first time, the men truly believed that there would be a game.

The British NCO in charge of a work party snapped to attention and tossed a salute to Colby.

"Good morning, Sergeant."

"Good morning, sir. How's the team coming?"

"Looking good, Sergeant. Looking real good."

"Will we beat Jerry, sir?"

"We're going to kick their balls so hard, they'll leave the field as sopranos!"

"Righto, sir." The man laughed. "Sopranos indeed, sir." The men in the work party joined their Sergeant in laughter.

"Good luck, sir," said one.

"Good luck," said another.

Colby lightly saluted them. "Thank you," he said and walked to the hut where he stopped and stared lovingly at the structure.

Waldron glared out of his window. For some perverse reason, fate had chosen the new player's hut to be constructed in clear view of the Senior British Officer's quarters. The sight offended him and every nail driven into the wood seemed to be driven into him personally.

"I wish they'd finish the bloody thing and get it over and done with," he muttered. "If it's the last thing I ever do, I'll see that that collaborator Colby gets what's coming to him. If there's any justice, the beggar'll be put in irons and shot." He slammed the table hard with his hand. "Shot, do you hear?"

Sherlock shrugged. "I wouldn't exactly call him a collaborator, sir. Colby's a lot of things, but a collaborator, no."

Waldron whirled at him. "And what do you call this exhibition in Paris? They're going to be exhibited like performing fleas. If that's not collaboration, what is it then?"

The hammering outside seemed to intensify. The colonel turned to the sound then back to his officers. "I don't think London is going to take very kindly to this, you know. I think their reaction is going to be precisely mine."

Rose's ears perked at the word "London." He was the intelligence officer and he knew of no camp connection with England.

"You've informed London?"

"No need, Phillip. The German propaganda machine will take care of that. They're no fools, you know. What the devil do you think this is all about . . . sportsmanship!?"

Captain James Lawry toyed with intricately carved pieces of tin. His bifocals were pushed to the edge of his nose, he hummed a snatch of an old Canadian woodsman's song and looked for all the world like a Gipetto creating a Pinocchio out of old biscuit and sardine tins. As a civilian, Lawry had been what was quickly becoming a dying breed of craftsman—a watchmaker. He would start with bits of high tempered steel and sterling and would fashion every intricate moving part of the timepiece by hand. It took Lawry a year, sometimes two, to complete one of his masterworks. It was this patience and skill that placed him in a commando unit as a demolitions expert.

Working directly under the command of Pyrie, James Lawry was the camp's master forger, clothing designer, and maker of gadgets. He fitted the last piece of tin together and admired his work. It was primitive, yes, but it was a camera that did the job, and that's what really counted.

Lawry and Hatch had been taken together at Dieppe, and Lawry was committed to helping his comrade in his fifth attempt to escape.

There was a respectful knock at the door. Lawry called out, "Come in, Bobby, you're expected."

Hatch popped his head into the room. "Hi ya', Jimmy boy. How's it going?"

"It's going well, Bobby. Are you ready?"

"Ready as rain, baby. Ready and raring to go. What have you got for me."

"A double-breasted blue serge, circa 1939."

Hatch rubbed his hands together. "Boy," he said, "I look beautiful in blue. I look beautiful in anything that ain't this god damn olive drab crap."

"Yes, you're gorgeous," Lawry agreed. "Now, let me look at you." He quickly surveyed Hatch. "Shave? Yes. Good. Hair? Mmmm, good." Then he gave his final pronouncement. "I think you'll make it. You already look like a Paris hotshot. You'll make it. Now go and get dressed."

Bobby took his time getting into the new outfit. He admired the handiwork on the white shirt.

"Flower sacks," Lawry said.

Hatch slipped into the trousers. They were baggy in the rear, but otherwise fit perfectly. He put on the coat, stretched, flexed his muscles, and grinned like a stroked Cheshire cat.

"God, does this feel good. Do you have a mirror?"

"No, sorry old man," James said. "You'll just have to take my word for it. You're gorgeous." Then he became professional. "Get over there by the window. It's time for your photo."

As Bobby posed in the shaft of the afternoon light, Lawry adjusted the tin machine. He rested it on a table top, focused it, then clamped the apparatus down.

"Did you make that?" Hatch asked.

"Uh huh." Lawry murmured.

"Well, you're a fucking genius," Bobby said.

"Put me down for two watches. No, make it three. I want to send one to the Smithsonian."

"Shut up and look depressed."

Bobby's face fell.

"That's it, that's it. Hold it." There was a loud click, and Lawry sighed. "You're immortalized."

"One more for luck."

"The films too valuable, Bobby, but don't worry, it's as good as any other passport photo." He crossed the small room and beckoned Hatch to him. "Now, Dupin's the name you want?"

"Yeah," Hatch said, "Marcel Dupin, electrician. And I'll need an address in Lyons."

"You'll have it." He was suddenly very professorial. "And why does Monsieur Dupin want to go home?"

"Compassionate leave. Poppa dropped dead. Can you do it?"

"Ha," Lawry said in a grand but very phony French accent, "I might, monsieur, even manage a letter on your bereavement. Bon?"

"Bon," Bobby answered.

Lawry pulled a hair brush from its hiding place beneath his bed. He slid the bristles back and proudly showed Bobby a rather fine and varied collection of stamps.

"Now, let me see. What have we got?" He looked at the stamp faces. "French police, entry into Germany, health officer, military district." He looked at Hatch in dismay and clucked his tongue. "Military district, they keep changing that—very inconsiderate."

"How long will it take?"

"Be patient, Bobby. It's my busy season. Everybody wants to escape in good weather. Just be patient."

"Patient!" Hatch howled. "Jesus Christ! I'm losing hair now. If I get any more patient, I'll be bald as a cue ball. Help me, Jimmy. Don't send me home scared." He broke into peals of anxiety-relieving laughter and the watchmaker joined him.

Hatch whistled his way out of the forger's hut, wound his way around the milling prisoners, and stationed himself in front of the area dearest to his heart: the wash house.

The forty men were marched like clockwork into the compound; but there was something different about them, something was radically wrong. Bobby's pulse rate increased, sweat formed on his brow. He tossed his head from right to left trying to shake the image.

"Who the fuck are those guys?"

The faces of the guards were as foreign as Martians. More than a year of desperate planning was going quickly down the drain.

He had one more shot. Maybe, just maybe, the new guards would be just as fucked up as the old reservists they replaced. He watched until all the men were led into the wash room, then he spun around, nauseous with frustration. The guards were different. They did their job, they patrolled like trained animals.

Hatch burst into the hut with such vehemence that the men inside bolted upright.

Sherlock slipped his glasses on. "What is it, Hatch?"

He paced the small room, then he turned on the men. "They've . . . they've switched guards on me.

The bastards are outside the wash house like they're supposed to be!"

Sherlock's voice was soft, apologetic. "I know."

"What do you mean, you know?" Hatch stomped over to him.

It took all of Sherlock's nerve to look into the fierce eyes. "The guards you depended on, Hans and Anton, have been switched to watch over Colby's football team."

Hatch wailed like a banshee. "But they're my goons. I practically invented them." He began to pace again, the madness still in his eyes. "Colby, that son of a bitch," he ranted. "He stole my goons." Then, addressing no one in particular, "I was ready to go. A blue suit, a good story, all my papers." He slammed a fist into the wall. "Jesus Q. Christ, I was almost over the fucking wall!"

"Bad luck," Sherlock said; "but between you and me, Hatch, I never thought it a very good plan."

"Bullshit," Hatch said, "I could have made it. I know I could have."

He swallowed hard and fought back the tears of despair.

CHAPTER EIGHT

The falcon was a beautiful graceful thing in a pale blue cloudless sky. It moved quickly, effortlessly, as it rode the wind and thermals. It dropped about 100 yards, and suddenly out of nowhere, a black bird about a quarter of its size attacked. The hawk, surprised, dipped its wings in a defensive maneuver, but the angry black dot pecked and dove with incredible speed into the confused and frightened hunter. Colby watched transfixed, and for a moment, he imagined himself behind the stick of his Lancaster. He heard the high whine of the Messerschmitts and could smell the cordite of bullets. He shouted, "Get out! Get out!", but his clenched teeth locked the scream tightly in his mind.

In seconds, the birds had disappeared into the strong glare of the midday sun. John turned away and stared at the empty new barracks; he inhaled the pleasingly pungent odor of new wood ready to absorb the sound and smell of man.

He pulled the dossier of players from the small desk that was set up next to a window, and in minutes he had forgotten the combat. The list he had compiled had the names of some of the most desirable footballers in the world.

"Maybe," he smiled as he mused, "just maybe, the conquered territories have more talent than Von Steiner or the higher ups at the Propaganda Ministry believed. Maybe their concept of the unbeatable Nietzschean superman is the Nazi fatal flaw. Maybe I will, indeed, kick their fucking balls in."

There was a hard knock at the door and he slipped the dossier into the desk's drawer before he answered it.

"Come in, gentlemen."

Four enlisted men entered carrying their kit bags. Of the fifteen thousand prisoners of war at Gensdorf, they were the only ones that had been chosen to play the German National team. In a day or so, from camps all over occupied Europe, the rest of those chosen would arrive. But for the moment, this palatial barren room was theirs and theirs alone.

"My God, man," the Calypso voice of Fernandez sang, "a governor's mansion."

"It's the bloody Savoy," Sid Harmer said.

"Damn right it is," Arthur Hayes parroted.

Terry Brady just stared. He had just spent three weeks in solitary confinement, and the barracks appeared gargantuan.

"From here on out, don't bother to knock," Colby said as he walked to them. "It's your home."

"Home? It's more like heaven." The voice boomed from the doorway and the men turned as Bobby Hatch entered lugging his kit bag and ready to move in. "I almost forgot what it was like to be a jock. 'Pampered and pussied' my old roomie used to say. 'That's what all you jocks get, pampered and pussied.' " His innocent eyes moved around the room. "Get any yet?"

"What the hell are you doing here, Hatch?"

"Why, John boy, I decided to join your team."

Colby dragged the chair out from behind the desk and looked at the brawny American.

"Oh? Do tell me everything."

"Well, being on the team is a one way ticket out of here, right?"

John shook his head. "You're not on this team, Hatch."

"Sure I am." The brown eyes stared intently. "I'm your new trainer."

"My what?"

"Your trainer. Maybe I can't play your kind of football, but if you play my kind, you know all there is to know about bruises, sprains and charley horses." Then he raised his hands and became a holy-rolling preacher. "I can heal, I can save, I can lay on the hands and make you whole again!"

Colby smiled and Hatch knew he had, at the very least, dented the man's armor. He took another tack. "Come on, Colby, you can do it. Speak to Von Steiner."

The players remained at the far end of the room, but their attention was with the two officers.

"Come on, Colby," Hatch urged again, "I'm a ball player. I don't want to be left out of something like this."

"Bullshit!" Colby said, and he meant it. "All you want is a chance to run for the wire."

Hatch's face dropped and, for a split second, Colby thought he looked small, vulnerable.

"So?" Bobby said. "Even if I do, isn't that my choice?"

"Not when you're using my team as a vehicle to do it. Besides, I don't want you getting killed."

"We're in the god damned army and getting killed is part of our business." His voice was strong now, angry. "And don't give me that 'my team' crap. It's you and your team that wrecked my escape. The whole thing depended on Anton and Hans and now those two goons are playing water boy for your team."

Colby thought on it for what seemed like a long time, then said, "Okay, you're on. But one fuck up, just one, and you're back to the hut with those six other cretins. Got it?"

"Got it." Hatch was grinning. "And you've got yourself the best god damned trainer this side of Gensdorf prison."

The tower guards at the main gate were as curious as they were cautious when the hooded truck, accompanied by two motorcycles and a small troop carrier, approached the prison. Both the officer of the day and Kommandant Willinger were issuing orders, and in minutes the truck had been cleared and was winding its way through the camp towards the players' compound.

Both Anton and Hans were at attention when Oberstleutnant Strauss and the British Captain Colby approached the truck. The oberstleutnant spoke sharply and the soldiers moved to his command. "Empty the truck!"

They tossed the canvas back and the guards who had made the dark, tedious trip with the prisoners were the first out. They squinted into the glare of the afternoon sun, spotted the officer, and by reflex stumbled into a semblance of a line.

Anton moved quickly to the truck and shouted, *"Heraus! Heraus! Schnell! Schnell!"*

And the men climbed down. The daylight seemed to bleed them of color. Even the dark green of their new fatigues played black against the stark white of their skins. The world of war was written into their faces, into the postures they assumed, the way they looked at the drab nothingness of the new camp that spread before them.

"Yes," Colby thought, "it's all there. Hate, misery, doubt, defiance, defeat. No wonder Von Steiner is so damn confident. What in hell could make these men a team?"

He handed the guard beside him the clipboard that listed the men, then he looked to the oberstleutnant, who nodded, and Hans called the roster.

"Morell."

The man stepped forward and, as he had done a hundred thousand times before, snapped to attention.

Colby shook his head. "This won't do, this won't do at all," he said to himself. Then he called, "At ease, men. Stand at ease."

The men instantly relaxed and all eyes moved to the blond man. Colby looked at their faces, then he stepped forward and smiled at a very familiar face.

"Tony, how are you?"

The man studied him closely, his brows knitted as his mind ran the maze of memory, then he ventured a tenuous smile.

"John? Is that really you?"

Colby moved to the soldier, and like very old and dear friends, they embraced.

"What's going on?" Tony whispered, as if afraid that his full voice would destroy the fragile reality of the moment.

"You'll know soon enough," Colby said. He affectionately rapped his shoulder and faced the next man. "You're Doug Clure, aren't you?"

"Yes, sir, I am."

"The name is Colby. John Colby. Welcome aboard."

John stopped in front of the next man, uncertain as to his identity.

"Remy," the man said without being asked. "John-Paul Remy."

"Vous êtes français?"

"Oui," the man answered.

"Bon," said John. *"Bon."*

And so he met the team.

Michel Filieu, Belgian ... Gunner Nilsson, Norwegian ... Erik Borge, Danish ... Pieter van Beck, a Dutchman ... and Carlos Rey, an Argentinian who served with the French Foreign Legion.

It would be a hard, tough pull, but he liked them. He liked what they radiated and he knew that if he could put their feelings of defeat and defiance together, it would spell "Victory."

"Come inside, gentlemen," he said. "We'll get something to eat and I'll explain it all."

Even if the ride in the darkened back of the truck hadn't taken twelve hours, even if they had been fed more than just a pint of water during the tedious trip, the men would still have been ravenous. To them, the meal of stew, bread, and beer was a feast.

The men wiped their bowls clean with swabs of black bread, then one by one, they leaned back, relaxed, waiting.

Hatch, like a beardless Santa, entered with a kit bag slung across his shoulder and a "Ho, ho" look in his eye.

"Okay, you guys, get happy." He passed from man to man and tossed them each a fresh package of American "Luckies." "Smoke 'em, or trade 'em," he called out.

Colby tapped the edge of the table with his hand. He made sure his eyes met every man at the table. "As you know, we're going to play football. We're going to play against the Hun, and we're going to beat them. We still respond to roll call three times a day, but apart from that we make our own rules. There will be no rank here. This is a football team, and I'm the only one you answer to. I'm the captain, the manager, and the war minister." He kept silent for a short while, then asked, "Any questions?"

Tony Morell lifted his glass. "I don't know how you did it, Johnny, but here's to victory."

And everyone joined in the chorus. "To victory!"

The Frenchman, Remy, sat at the edge of his cot and, as if he were in a trance, rocked back and forth as he spoke in a deeply passionate voice. "I need a gun, Captain, or a knife. Will you get that for me?" The sudden silence counterpointed the drama of the moment. "Right now my people are in the mountains. Like animals, they live in caves and forests, hunting and being hunted. I come from generations of vintners. Our wine press is seven hundred years old." Remy stared at his boots. His movements, hypnotic with their steady, slow meter, held the team entranced.

"I played in Paris. We lost, but I was a hero because I'd seen Paris. . . . I played in Paris. None of my family had ever been to a big city before."

He looked around the room, his eyes moving chillingly from face to face. "Now my village is gone. The church that saw the ocean is an outpost for artillery. First the soldiers came, and, like all soldiers on the move, they stole and raped; and when they moved on, the SS came and killed and packed the children and women into freight cars." He drew a breath and hissed it loudly through his lips. "No one lives in that little piece of Normandy now. No one. It is a place of ghosts and tanks. And you ask me to touch those men on a pitch and not kill them, you ask me to play a game with rules." He rose and shouted, "Captain, get me a gun! Captain, get me a knife! Captain, get me a wire to strangle with!"

Then he sat and tears ran unabashedly down his cheeks.

The outburst purged him. In the morning he was ready for the workout.

With every stride, the men sobbed into the chilled air. Sweat stained black against their cumbersome military clothing, glistened on their puffed faces. John jogged with the men as they ran the makeshift track that circled the pitch. Tony Morell slowed and John shouted, "Move!

Move your bleedin' arse, you third rate malingering son of a bitch!"

Morell turned a sweat-streaked face, glared his anger, then twisted back to the running men and picked up his pace.

Colby never knew a good player who liked this phase of the game, who liked being pushed by anyone. They were too strong, too individualistic, and he was inwardly delighted at Morell's anger.

Van Beck broke stride, slowed, limped to the sideline, and Hatch was instantly beside him.

"What's the matter, baby?"

The Dutchman shook his head. "It is nothing, nothing."

"Let me take a look." Bobby bent, touched the ankle, and the man pulled back with a gasp of pain.

"What's the matter, Pieter?" Bobby asked again. This time there was concern in his voice.

The Dutchman looked into the brown eyes. "When I was taken in Amsterdam, the Gestapo . . ." His voice trailed off for a moment. "My legs, they twisted my legs, and sometimes they hurt me very much."

"Why don't you go on up to the hut and take it easy for a while? Tonight I'll rub you down and wrap you up nice like." Bobby forced a smile. "I'm pretty good, you know."

"Thank you," Pieter said, "but I've got to try. I can do it."

He turned, hobbled to the track, drew a deep breath and began a slow painful jog.

CHAPTER NINE

If it was psychological warfare that Von Steiner was conducting, it was effective. The German National team was better than good. They were fast, deadly on the offensive, and above all, they were in shape. Yes, they were topflight.

Colby tore his eyes away from the field and looked at Von Steiner who was beaming with pride as the Germans moved the ball downfield. Although it was a practice session, the intensity, the beauty of the coordinated effort was devastatingly clear to Colby's trained eye. He turned back to the field and watched as Helmut Rhinegold, the captain, burnt down the field and stole the ball. An opposition back moved to tackle, but Helmut spun with the ball, feinted to the right, and left the man falling as he shot through for a goal. It was masterful.

"Beautiful, beautiful," Kurt shouted.

Colby suddenly understood why Von Steiner had brought him to the training camp. "They're good, all right. Damned good," he said.

"Thank you," Kurt said modestly. Then he looked to the pitch where Helmut, the golden boy of the German National team, had only a trace of sweat on his face, the exertion of the practice session hardly noticeable. He stopped a few feet from the men and slowly, with a radiant smile, walked to them.

"Good afternoon, Major Von Steiner."

"Good afternoon, Helmut."

The player's eyes went immediately to Colby. "You are John Colby?"

"Yes, I am."

He extended his hand. "I am Helmut Rhinegold. A pleasure to meet you, Captain."

He was so handsome, so young, and his smile so disarming, that John took his hand and found himself saying, "My pleasure. You looked great out there."

"Thank you. But if your team is as good as Major Von Steiner says it is, we will have to get much better if we're to survive on the pitch with you."

"*Much* better," John replied.

"Good, good. I am delighted," Helmut countered. "We need a good game. Every team we play seems to fall apart. It's too easy, it takes the joy of winning out of it."

"Well," Colby said, with a grin, "I think that my boys will give you some grief, Captain."

"Perhaps, perhaps," Helmut said and then suddenly changed the subject. "I've seen your new uniforms, and I must say, they're striking."

"Oh?" said Colby.

"You'll be called 'The Cardinals of Gensdorf.' "

"Red?"

"Red. Yes;" the blond player said. "It was a special request on my part. I wanted the crowds in Paris to make sure they could see the team we've beaten."

"Or been beaten by," Colby said.

"That would be the fortunes of war, would it not, Captain?"

"Yes," John said. "The fortunes of war."

He was beginning to dislike the man. He had everything on his side, and yet he wanted more. "Everything, they want everything," Colby said to himself.

The handsome face smiled again. "Come to practice any time you like, Captain Colby. We always appreciate a good and appreciative crowd." He looked to Kurt. "*Auf wiedersehen,* Major."

"*Auf wiedersehen,*" Von Steiner said, and both men watched as Helmut raced across the field towards his waiting teammates.

"Confident, isn't he?" Colby said.

"Winners are that way, Captain."

"Yes, I suppose so. Did he really choose red as our color?"

"Yes, do you mind?"

"Mind? Hell, no." He beamed the lie through a huge false smile. "Red was my winning color when I played for Glasgow." He was beginning to enjoy the invention. "And remember, that was the year we took the national championship."

Michel stared down at his new playing boots, then looked across the room at the men who were pulling on the last of the flaming red uniforms. It was very much like the changing rooms all of them had experienced, but there was more excitement, more camaraderie that was as much a part of a team as the passing of a ball or a sensational kick. Only the air was too clean. It lacked the bite of linament and sweat, but this would come, and then they would smell like players, like a team.

"Could all of this really be happening?" He thought. "There is madness here. But when the American, Hatch, caught his eye, he smiled. He knew it was real. The team's trainer had a ball in his hand and bounced it on the floor, calling for their attention.

Bobby pulled an old basketball trick. He held the ball high and spun it on the tip of his index finger. He waited until he caught the eye of almost every man in the hut, then he tossed it.

With the honed instincts of the professional, Gunner Nilsson allowed the ball a bounce, then kicked it hard and high. The ball slammed into the ceiling, ricocheted into the wall and was immediately stopped and headed forward by Fernandez. Michel leapt, blocking the pass. The men kicked the empty boxes and fell over themselves laughing. The ball was in play, and the barracks was suddenly alive with the one thing they all understood . . . soccer.

One of the miracles of prison life is the rapidity with which information is spread. The prisoners knew about the arrival of the red suits before the first batch was unpacked, and they lined the wires waiting for the team to appear. There was a genuine excitement among most of the men that was not shared by either Rose or Sherlock. When the team jogged out onto the field and the men cheered, they remained impassive.

Bobby led the men for a turn around the track and, in a near perfect imitation of Colby, shouted over the friendly catcalls, "Take no notice, lads. They're only jealous." Holding an extended finger up to the heavens, he continued jogging and he chanted as he ran, "Up, up, up yours . . . up, up, up yours!"

Colby set up the exercise. He formed the men into a loose circle and headed the ball to Doug Clure.

"Doug!" he shouted. The man found the ball and headed it to Carlos Rey. "Yours, Carlos!" he called. And so it went for almost an hour, from head to head at the shout of a name.

Then they dribbled, passing the ball from right foot to left foot, and ran until exhausted, with Colby always beside them, pointing out a weakness, enhancing a strong point.

Hatch stood beside the goal and watched the men as they fired the ball into the net. He turned to Sherlock. "Pretty good, eh? The bastards are gonna have to go some to beat 'em."

Sherlock shrugged. "You're an optimist, Hatch."

"What's the matter with you, Sherlock? For crying out loud, be a human being. You know what's going on, you know everything. You know that one of the guys almost got his ankles busted off, and in spite of the pain he's playing a great game. They're all like that. We're all like that. We've all got something busted, but I'll tell you what ain't busted with those guys. That's lotsa balls and heart—a lotta heart . . ."

He was going to say more, he was going to say, "Now get the fuck off the field before I take you apart." But, just then, Colby called sharply, "Hatch!"

As Hatch turned, Colby fired a powerful lofting kick at him. By virtue of sheer natural reflex, Hatch turned and caught it.

"Bravo!" Colby shouted and the team applauded. "That's not bad at all."

"What do you mean, not bad? I'm terrific. Best pair of hands east of the Alps."

"Get over there," Colby said, pointing to the goal, "and let's see what you can do." He turned and shouted to Fernandez, "Luis, shoot him a hard one!"

Fernandez fired the ball towards the goal. Bobby leapt for a save and stopped the score. Then he flung the ball back into play.

"Okay, okay. You bums don't know who you're fooling with. This is Bobby Hatch, the last of the great goal . . ."

He never finished the sentence. Van Beck dribbled the ball towards the goal. He faked a shot, Bobby dove for it, and Pieter tapped it into the other side of the net.

Hatch shouted from his prone position on the ground, "Hey, Pieter, I thought you were my friend!"

"I am your friend. To be fair, Bobby, you don't dribble well, you don't kick well, but you have good hands. You could be a good goalkeeper."

"He's right, Hatch," Colby added. "If you kept training, you'd be damn good."

"I wouldn't be a goalkeeper if my life depended on it. The job stinks."

"Why?"

"Look," Hatch said, sounding perfectly reasonable, "you stand around all day doing nothing, and when the team loses, whose fault is it?" He looked around for a reply, then answered himself. "The goalkeeper's. Forget it. I don't want the responsibility."

Colby looked at him in sheer exasperation. "Hatch," he said, "take a god damned cold shower. Do anything, but get out of my sight!"

"Consider me gone," Hatch said. "All gone!"

Waldron cleared his throat and stared directly into Colby's eyes. "You've spent a considerable amount of time with that Von Steiner," he said. "What do you make of him?"

"I would say that Major Rose here would probably know more about him than I, sir. I don't think he's a Nazi, but they've given him a fairly free hand with this thing so he must be good for the bastards." He shrugged. "So far, he's come through with most of his promises, and as much as anyone can trust an enemy, I trust Von Steiner."

The colonel shook his head ever so slightly before he replied. "I'll be perfectly frank with you, Captain Colby. I don't like the smell of this thing. It reeks of betrayal. They won't let you win. A victory would be a great coup for them, and a defeat an equally great disgrace. They won't let you win even if you had a chance."

John found his voice harden. "I have a chance, Colonel, and I think we can beat them."

Rose was on his feet. "I'm afraid I agree with Colonel Waldron. There's no way they are going to let you win. I think you ought to cancel this match."

The hardness in Colby's voice was becoming flinty. "I think not," he said. "I'm going to play this game."

Waldron played what he thought was his trump card. "How do you think London will react to this? It is, in a sense, consorting with the enemy. It might even be considered treacherous."

"Frankly, Colonel, I don't give a fucking god damn how London will react, and anyone who is stupid enough to think me a traitor can bloody well kiss my arse!" He was into it now. He felt exhilarated by the release of emotion. "I've been a prisoner for almost three years and I hate it. Perhaps when the war is over I'll think differently about it, but just now, Colonel, I hate prison worse than death. I hate being caged, I hate not being able to hit back. But I can fight on the playing field, and even if I lose, the bastards will know they had a battle. I'm going to play this game and nothing is going to fucking stop me!"

He whirled and left the room.

Waldron was on his feet shouting, the veins in his neck and temples throbbing. Sherlock had never seen Waldron in such a maddened state. This show of hysteria, coming from a man who had spent most of his career in diplomatic circles, appalled and frightened him.

"I'm the Senior Officer here and when I give a command, it will be obeyed!" He turned to Rose, his voice rising. "I'll have him shot, do you hear? As the Lord is my witness, I'll have that bastard shot!"

CHAPTER TEN

John Colby's squadron had been lucky in its first missions. They had supported the American invasion of Sicily and had sustained a minimum of casualties. Then there were milkruns over North Africa.

But Germany, the first strikes at the Nazi heartland, was a different story. Neither the British Spitfire nor any of the American fighters carried enough fuel to support their deep penetration missions, and they faced the Messerschmitts 109's with whatever firepower the Lancasters carried themselves. That any of the squadron survived the first three runs over Hanover and Cologne, that they rode through the black clouds of flak that tossed them with gale force and tore through the men and machines with deadly accuracy—this was, to Colby, a major miracle. The statistics of the first flights were a blur to him. A 60 percent loss, then 65 percent, then a lucky 40.

The target was Stuttgart. John Perry was the first to be hit. A painter, a sculptor, a good friend, a hard drinker, a splendid co-pilot. A bit of ack-ack tore through the top of the fuselage and took the right side of his head and neck and shoulder before it imbedded somewhere in the aircraft. An oil line severed in his port engine, and the bearings screamed loud enough for John to hear them over the battle sounds. The engine smoked and the prop ground to a halt. The Lancaster fell, and John slammed the starboard throttle forward as far as it would go and pulled back on the stick. They were losing altitude quickly. He feathered the port prop, compensated with a bank, and miraculously the ship began to climb. As if it were the inner workings of his mind, the intercom came alive, roaring pain and confusion.

"Jackson . . . Jerry at 3 o'clock!"

A cry of pain, the ship shuddered as every gun spit bullets at the attacking Messerschmitts.

"John!" Karinski, the bombardier, cried. "Losing target—bring her down—bring her down!"

"Unload, Karinski!" Colby brushed the sweat and John Perry's blood off his face and brow. "Unload, we're losing sky fast! Unload!"

"Roger," Karinski answered and released the bombs.

Tense voices dominated the intercom.

"This is the Captain. Clear the line!"

It took a moment for the babble to subside.

"Jettison everything! Everything except your parachutes. Do you read me? Everything!'

The crew responded with quiet hysteria. They tore instruments from riveted plates, tossed bandoliers of .50 caliber ammo, then the bomb sight. Gunners loosened their weapons and pushed them into the slipstream. Everything went out the open hatch except the bodies of the dead. No one, not even the most fearful of the crewmen, thought them cargo.

They touched down twenty-eight minutes behind squadron, literally more dead than alive.

John Perry was staring at Colby with one good eye, parts of his brain sliding down his cheek.

John shouted at the top of his lungs, "What? What is it, Perry? What is it?"

He bolted upright, staring at the foreign room outlined by the full moon. He was naked, convulsed in malarial tremble, sweat glistened on his quivering body. The nightmare lingered, then faded. Only a sense of horror held.

The knocking began gently, and when John didn't respond, it roughened in its intensity.

"Yes?" Colby demanded angrily. "Who the devil is it?"

"It's me." Bobby entered without being asked. "Team's waiting."

He looked closely at Colby then walked to him. "You all right? You sick or something?"

The nightmare was still partially imbedded in John's mind, and he shook his head trying to release it.

"No, I'm all right. I'm fine."

"Well, you look like shit."

"Thank you. I really appreciate that."

"Don't mention it," Bobby said with a smile. "Always ready to help any way I can. Come on, saddle up, the guys are waiting for you."

Colby got dressed and moved quickly into the

main room. The cots, pushed away from the walls, formed a semicircle around him. It was the squad's first strategy session, and the men were attentive.

"Okay, now I want you to listen closely," he began. "We all want to go out there looking flashy and make them look like the low lifes they are. But that's exactly their thinking—and if we get sucked into their game plan, it's all over, we haven't a chance."

Now all eyes were on him.

"I've seen the Germans play and they're really fit. They're very strong. The reality is that we're in no condition to run for ninety minutes. If we play a running game they will stamp us into the ground and we will be lucky to lose by ten to one. One bit of grandstanding and we're finished."

They were listening now and John knew that this was the turning point. He held his pause a few seconds longer then continued. "All right then. Backs, when you see the winger coming down, get down and hold him close. Really stay with him and that'll save you running, because you're not. I repeat, not in any state to run. Don't try anything physical. Just stay close with them. Don't try and be a hero and get a goal yourself. I want you to pass, always pass. Let the ball do the running for you."

He walked back to the wall and with bold lines marked their places on the primitive diagram.

"Just remember this. When you get to here," he pointed to the right winger's position, "if you can get a corner, that will be our advantage. We've a set piece, we've time for everybody not to stroll up, but we can go up, we don't have to run up. Remember this, and I mean remember it. Any chance we can get to stand still, take it." Colby leaned back against the wall. "I know that there are a great many questions, but most of the answers will have to be worked out on the pitch."

The men began to stir, but John held them.

"Just a minute, gentlemen. I've got some good news." The hut fell to silence. "I've asked for some East European players and tomorrow I expect delivery. I think you'll be surprised as to who they are, and maybe they can give us that extra bit of strength we need. Here's the list... Gregor Mikaholovich." There was a murmur of approval. "Milos Freemun."

"Jesus Christ!"

"No, not Jesus Christ, just Milos Freemun."

"Damn near the same," Sid said. "I played against that monster."

"And Laszlo Nevax and Janos Rachivski," John added.

"Jerry must be crazy giving those guys to us," Tony said. "That's heavy artillery."

"Yeah," Colby said with a smile, "maybe the counteroffensive has begun. Good night, gentlemen, sleep well."

John leaned up against the hut. The barracks behind him was still humming with the sound of the excited squad. The men felt good, but he felt terrific. He felt like a winner.

With prods of rifle butts, the East Europeans were driven from the rear of the truck, like animals. They were incapable of making the leap from the truck to the ground and stood staring at nothing, their cheeks hollowed, their heads shaved.

The squad had planned a welcome for these

players, had pooled their cigarettes for them to smoke or use as currency. They had tins of beef and sardines to offer. They planned handshakes and smiling hellos, but the sight of the new arrivals struck the players dumb, made them feel ashamed of their new strength and red uniforms, forced them to remember that they were prisoners and that this was war.

Hatch was the first to recover. "Hello," he said. Then he paused as he searched for words. "Do any of you speak English?" One of them nodded. "I'm Robert Hatch. I'm a captain in the Canadian Army."

The man stared at him, then flinched, and Bobby saw the lice.

He led them towards the showers with a gentle voice. "Come, come with me. Come." And they followed him.

Colby turned to the man closest to him. "Doug, give him a hand."

The Scotsman moved immediately, and three of the team followed. John looked after them and shouted, "I've got some DDT in my hut. Use it, then burn their clothes."

The men silently wandered back into the barracks. Colby stood alone, pondering the fate of the broken men. He looked up and saw Rose and Sherlock approaching.

"Well, old chap," Rose said, "looks as if Von Steiner has guaranteed his win in Paris. It was rather clever of him to send you those four skeletons."

"I asked for them," John said.

Rose's brow lifted. "You? But why?"

"They're all great players."

"You mean they were. "Don't you see..."

Then he shook his head. "It's no use. There's no way to get through to you. I understand that, but that isn't the reason I'm here."

"No?"

"No. We've picked up the BBC, and London is very much aware of this fiasco. It's in all the papers. London is calling it another German lie. They're saying no British officer would be involved in such a scheme."

"London is saying? What about those poor bastards there? If I call this game off they'll be sent back to whatever hell they've been brought out of. What the hell do I do about them?"

"That," said Rose with a great deal of self-satisfaction, "is for you to work out." He moved his cold blue eyes up to Colby's. "Another thing is what you're going to do about the BBC's broadcast. It's not official, of course, but the message is clearly what the Colonel said it would be, and that is that this game borders on collaboration. I think, Colby, that that is something you have to put before your men. I know you're willful, but this must be a decision every man must come to by themselves. Don't you think so?"

Their shrunken stomachs would not hold down the meal the squad had prepared for them, and the men, in the overly large fatigues the team scrounged for them, ate slowly, mincing their food. The room was silent; none of the jubilation of the night before was evident in the hut.

John pushed his tin plate away from him and cleared his throat. When he got to his feet, all eyes were upon him. "Gentlemen," he began, "the BBC has, in effect, denounced this game. They feel that this is a German propaganda offensive and that we're playing into their hands." He scratched his chin. "All of us, I'm sure, agree with the first part of the announcement. This is clearly what Jerry accepts. What London doesn't, and couldn't know, is that we have a team here and that we can possibly beat the Hun at their own game. At least," he said softly, "I truly believe so."

He pointed to the new men. "I insisted on having these men, so the responsibility for them is mine and mine alone. I can't tell you to disobey either your consciences or the orders of government; thus the decision as to whether we play or not is yours."

Colby's words reached out into the room, touching each and every man with the choice and challenge of free will. It was an experience most of them had not had in years, and it left them silent, pondering.

Jean-Paul leaned to Michel and they spoke quickly with many gestures. They nodded in agreement, and Remy rose.

"Captain Colby," he shifted from foot to foot like an embarrassed boy. "Michel and I, we have decided. We play. There seems to be no other choice."

John nodded his thanks, then his eyes wandered over the faces of the other men. The cold, bare bulb that hung over them cast strange shadows and the shadows made masks of their faces. There was doubt and mirth, a glance that had the look of either cunning or wisdom, and then there was defiance. The Scotsman, Doug Clure, spoke out. "Yes, I agree," he said in his deep Highland burr. "We play!"

Then, one by one, with nods of the head and

waves of the arms, the men voted "for Paris." Only Hatch seemed to defer. He leaned against the far barracks wall, his arms crossed, and he smiled as all eyes turned to him. The pose was overtly theatrical, and he savored the moment before he spoke.

"I vote for Paris," he said; "but you guys are going without me. I just got word from Pyrie that my stuff is ready and I'm going over the wall!"

Bobby stuck his head into the forger's room. He had slicked his hair back and parted it almost in the center. In his mind, he absolutely believed he was Parisian.

"*Bonjour*, Captain Lawry."

James looked up, smiling. "*Bonjour*, Monsieur Dupin. *Ça va?*"

"*Bien merci*," Hatch said. "How's that for an accent?"

"I've heard worse, believe me. What else can you say?"

"*Je vais à un enterrement.*" Then he translated brightly. "I'm going to a funeral." He pulled a chair and sat beside his friend. "It won't get me laid, but it might get me by the Germans."

"Might," Lawry agreed.

"You got my papers?"

"They're finished, yes, but the escape committee has them. They want to see you."

"Yeah, what about?"

James shrugged. "I haven't the foggiest, old man."

Bobby sensed a problem. He searched Lawry's eyes. "Anything wrong?"

"Not from this end, no."

"I don't know," Bobby said, rising. "I don't trust those sons of bitches."

Lawry rose with him. "They're all right. They know what their doing and they mean well."

"Yeah, I suppose you're right," Bobby said, and he started for the door. "Take care."

"You take care. And Bobby, remember to carry your identity tags when you go. I don't want you to be shot as a spy."

"I don't want to be shot as anything, and I'm not gonna. By the time intelligence gets through debriefing me, the fucking war will be over and I'll be in London for the celebration."

"Right," Lawry said. "That's the spirit."

Bobby waved. *"Au revoir."*

"Au revoir," the forger echoed, *"Et bonne chance, mon ami."*

When his friend left, James Lawry sat back and watched particles of dust dance in the sliver of light that beamed into his room. He was worried about the American, worried that Waldron and the escape committee wanted to see him. It was not their modus operandi. Something was wrong with the plan.

"Cup of tea?" Waldron asked.

"Tea?" Bobby repeated. This was the last thing in the world he had expected to hear, but he nodded. "Yes, thank you."

Pyrie poured while Waldron toyed with a string-bound package that contained Hatch's papers. The colonel pulled the counterfeit passport and admired it.

"Beautiful. That Lawry is a genius. God only knows what the fellow will do in civilian life." He toyed with the little blue book. "Make his own pound notes, I shouldn't wonder." He smiled at his own little joke then paused, waiting for someone else to pick up the conversation.

"Are you ready to go?" Pyrie asked.

"Yeah, pretty near." Hatch was becoming increasingly uncomfortable. He wanted to grab his papers and run. Instead he said, "I—I would like to thank you all very much."

"Oh, it's all part of the game, old man," Waldron said. "Team work, you know. Helping one another is the most important part of the whole thing."

"Yeah, I suppose so." He noticed Waldron's hand covering the passport and various official papers, and he knew then that he wasn't getting out of that room until they were good and ready to let him out.

"How would you like to do something for us, Hatch—providing, of course, that you do get beyond the wires?"

"This is it," Hatch thought, "the knife is falling."

"Sure," he said, then hedged, "anything I can."

Sherlock was instantly alert and fired the first question. "Which way were you planning to go?"

"To Lyon, then over the Swiss border."

"Switzerland, eh?" Rose said slyly. "I suppose you haven't thought of going by Paris?"

All the alarms went off at once, and he began to sweat. "Paris? No, no I hadn't thought of Paris. Word has it that the place is swarming with Gestapo hunting down the Resistance. The place is supposed to be dirty with them."

Rose ignored his words completely. "You'd find

it easier. They simply wouldn't expect you to go that way."

"And who could blame them?" Hatch said sarcastically. "A person would have to have brain damage to walk into that mess."

"Not quite true," Sherlock said. "We could supply you, with contacts, names, safe houses. I assure you, Hatch, you would be well looked after."

"I'll tell you the truth," Bobby said and felt his jaw tighten in determination. "I wasn't really planning on Paris until after the war."

He glanced down at the table where Waldron's hand still covered the documents. It was the move of a gambler. They wanted something from him, and unless he agreed, there would clearly be no escaping. It was table stakes, and the ante was clearly his freedom.

"All right, Colonel," he said, "what do you want?"

"We'd like you to contact the Resistance for us."

"Why?"

Sherlock played the next card. "Our plan is to arrange for the escape of the football team. All of them, the whole team."

With his no-nonsense tone of voice, Waldron leapt onto the tail end of Sherlock's statement. "Colby, as you know, is not going to let go of this ridiculous game of his, and we simply can't let the Germans succeed. Don't you see, Hatch? It's a wonderful opportunity for us to turn the tables on them. To make this stunt work for us."

"Why send me?" Hatch said, suddenly weary. "The French may have thought of all this themselves."

"Indeed, they may," Sherlock said, "but then again, they may not. We have to get word to them somehow."

Bobby looked down at the long feminine fingers that held claw-like to his papers. "What do you want me to do?"

"Find out whether an escape is feasible," Waldron said quickly.

"And if it isn't?"

"Then it isn't," the colonel said with a tinge of impatience. "If you reach them, the worst that can happen is they'll get you to Spain or Switzerland, or they'll hole you up until this bloody thing is over."

Bobby hesitated, and Rose, using his soothing tones, played his last card. "It's not asking much, old man. You know the team, you know who and what they are. If the Resistance buys the proposition, you'll be indispensable to the operation."

"All right," Hatch said in almost a whisper, "I'll do it."

"Good." Waldron smiled and pushed the packet forward. "We knew we could count on you."

"I'll go over the details with you tonight," Rose offered, "but remember, not a word to Colby."

"Holy Christ, fellas," Hatch said, "give the guy a break. He'll have to know something."

"Not necessarily," Sherlock chirped. "Not until it's a reality."

Bobby stuffed the papers into the top of his trousers. "You know, I really don't believe this, any of this. This stupid fucking game is wrecking my life."

When he was gone, the committee began to

relax. This round of play was theirs. Rose noticed the brimming mug on the table and mirthfully looked to his colonel. "He didn't drink his tea, sir," he said.

CHAPTER ELEVEN

The squad was behaving like schoolboys. Carlos, whom the men had dubbed "The Crazy Argentinian," had pumped a dead ball full of air and headed it to the front of the line. The action was about to create chaos when both Hans and Anton descended upon the field. The Germans were in a fury until Colby stopped the play. He caught the ball and threw it to Anton.

"All right, stop this horsing around and start behaving like soldiers, you bloody twits."

The guards loved the sound of the commanding voice and immediately understood that the British captain was as annoyed with these men as they were. Anton clutched the ball as if it were a trophy, scowled at the players, and smiled at John.

"Danke, Herr Kapitän," Hans said.

"Bitte," John sternly replied. Then he shouted.

"All right, you filthy thugs. On to the wash house."

Bobby caught his eye and they exchanged a quick affectionate smile.

Surrounded by the laughing, boisterous men, Hatch stripped naked. Although he was outwardly calm, his body glistened with sweat and the sound of his heart thumped in his ears. Janos, the emaciated Czechoslovakian, opened the overly large shirt that draped his body and unwound the blue serge suit. Milos, his partner, did the same with the flower sack shirt.

In the showers, Gunner Nilsson and Erik Borge started a water fight, and every man reacted to it with hoots and sprays of water.

"They're insane," Anton said to Hans. He wiped the water dripping from his chin and followed his companion out into the clear air of the enclosure.

Doug Clure knelt, waited for Hatch to mount his shoulders, and slowly he lifted the American. Bobby steadied his hand and began the slow and terrifying first step. This was his fifth attempt at escape and he knew he would probably spend the rest of the war in a five foot by seven foot solitary cell if he were seen now. He brought the long nosed pliers to the first of the staples that held a screen in place and started to pry. The first two held stubbornly, the rest almost fell by themselves.

Colby pulled out a box of "Players." He popped one into his mouth, then, as if remembering his manners, offered the box of cigarettes to the guards.

"Bitte?" John said, with an open, innocent face.

"Danke," Fritz said. He slung his old Mauser over his shoulder and lit up.

Bobby pushed the screen up, gripped the lip of the opening, and pulled himself into the darkness beyond. Then he reached down and Doug, who had wrapped the clothing into a loose knot, tossed them up into his waiting hands. Hatch looped a wire around the dislodged screen and pulled it back into position.

The men stood at attention and waited for Anton to call the roll. Oberstleutnant Strauss stood off to a side, clipboard in hand. He was aware of a restlessness among the prisoners. Time and time again his eyes slid over the assembled men, but whatever it was that disturbed him, it was elusive. That afternoon he had received his orders. He was being transferred, and he was facing this transfer with a mixture of pleasure and foreboding.

Anton called the roster of the footballers, but Strauss heard only half of the shouted names and the prisoners' replies.

"No matter," he thought to himself, "no one is leaving Gensdorf Prison this week." Then he smiled inwardly. "No one, that is, but Oberstleutnant Strauss."

"Van Beck, Pieter?"

"Here."

"Hatch, Robert?"

"Here."

"Filieu, Michel?"

And so it went until Strauss, satisfied, dismissed them.

Erik Borge turned to the soldier sandwiched

between himself and Gunner Nilsson and smiled broadly, but the man did not respond. Borge nodded to Nilsson, and together they walked him to the hut. The imperturbable man between was a perfectly formed dummy of Captain Robert Hatch.

Bobby waited for the sunlight that shone between the slats to fade, then dropped into the abandoned lavatory. In the deepening shadows, he could make out the objects Major Rose described. A broken toilet bowl, empty paint cans, worn brushes, newspapers. He peered out of the window, watched the guard making his rounds, and he counted.

Thirty-one, thirty-two, thirty-three, a pause at the wire and a turn. It was a perfect performance, and Bobby sighed with relief. He pushed his pick into the lock, held his breath and twisted. The mechanism moved so silently and so quickly that the weight of his leaning body almost thrust him out into the compound. He pulled back with a grunt. To silence the thunderous chattering of his teeth, he forced his open palms against his jaw.

John wandered to the window of his hut and studied the horizon. The sun dipped behind the trees, its rays colored the sky, and black clouds, like ships driven by a strong north wind, sailed silently across a yellow sea. He knew that Bobby, waiting for this moment, was watching the same creep of night. He closed his eyes and sent a thought across the naked prison ground.

"Good luck, Bobby. Good luck, my friend."

The guard was half way to the opposite wire when Hatch made his move. He gripped the bundle of clothes between his teeth, then slipped out of the door into the brightly lit yard and hefted himself up onto the roof.

Rose dealt himself his fifth hand of solitaire. He checked his watch and looked across the room to Sherlock, who stopped his pacing, turned, and stared at him. According to Hatch's schedule, he should be on the roof, naked, waiting to slip off the opposite end of the wash house into the German part of the prison. They knew he was cold and that there might be dogs.

Bobby lay flat on the roof. The music and laughter that came from the Kommandant's love nest turned his mind away from the bitter wind that lashed across his body. He was about to slip down into the enclosure and make his run for the dark end of the barrack where Willinger's auto waited, when he heard the guard approach.

The shepherd was no more than seven months old. Her ears were still flapped and her eyes bright and curious. She heeled to the guard's command, and when he jerked the leash and grunted, she stopped and sat. Then Hatch moved about a quarter of an inch and her ears perked. She woofed and wagged her tail. The guard drew a deep, impatient breath, murmured soft encouraging words, scratched her head, and moved on.

The girl sat on the Kommandant's lap in the back seat of his car. She had the top of his right boot in her hand and with a hard and final pull, she jerked the boot so that his feet slid into the soft black leather.

"Gut," Willinger said. *"Gut."* Then he gently swatted her backside with his swagger stick and the girl laughed.

The Kommandant's driver heard the laughter as it blended with the music, and his mind drifted to a town near Hamburg. He had a naked, dark-haired woman in his arms; the scent of her hair was very much like red roses.

When Hatch lay flat on the running board, the driver was moving his hands over the softness of his wife's shoulders, and he never felt the quiver of the automobile as it tilted slightly to his right.

The staff car started, then came to a stop at the main gate. The sentry threw his arm out in salute and walked to the idling Mercedes.

"Gut abend," he said to the familiar driver, then his eyes focused on the lady in the rear. She was very beautiful, and he gave her an embarrassed second look then saluted the Kommandant and passed the automobile through.

Bobby held on desperately as the car began to pick up speed. The road beneath him whirred by inches from his face. When the car slowed at a sharp curve, he pushed off and rolled into a fern-filled ditch. He lay there for minutes, amazed that he had taken the fall and was still alive. He ran through a mental checklist. Arms, legs, back, head, all okay, A-okay. He ran to the first stand of trees beside the road, untied the bundle, and slipped into the shirt and blue suit. He was tucking his papers into the breast pocket of the coat when he felt something that wasn't on his inventory. He pulled the soft thing out and strained to see what it was.

James Lawry, as a personal gift, had fashioned a beret out of an odd piece of cloth. Bobby's eyes filled with tears.

CHAPTER TWELVE

Hatch waited until he heard the train in the distance before he entered the depot. Fifteen or twenty people sat quietly or huddled in what appeared to be family groups. Hatch looked them over carefully. There were a few soldiers, a man he took to be a minor government official, and then he sighted his target: an old woman clutching the hand of a young boy. He glanced out onto the platform and in the weak light saw an officer standing beside his luggage, then he turned and walked to the ticket window.

"Paris," he said with a bad enough German accent so that the vendor would know he was a foreigner. "*Un billet pour Paris.*"

The whistle of the train brought all the passengers to their feet, and together they started for the platform. Bobby rushed to the old lady.

"Bitte?" he said with a smile and lifted her suitcase.

"Danke schön," the old lady replied and in appreciation showed a full mouth of missing teeth.

He helped the grandmother up the first high step, then he lifted the boy and placed him beside her. The railroad policeman touched his shoulder just as he was about to join them.

"Was is der grund ihrer reise?"

"Parlez-vous Français?" Bobby asked, flashing his idiot smile and handing the man his papers.

The policeman glanced at the passport and ignored the rest of the official-looking documents. He was openly suspicious of this man. He was too young, too tall and strong looking not to be in the army or with a labor battalion.

"Sprechen sie nicht Deutsch?"

"Non," Hatch said, and he knew that this was going to be the acid test for his funeral speech. *"Je vais à un enterrement à Paris."* He pointed to his black armband. *"Un enterrement."*

The wheel of the locomotive spun and the coaches clashed together, jarring both men.

"Bitte. Bitte. Le train," Hatch shouted with a genuine urgency. And for the life of him, he could not remember either the French or the German word for the departing steam breathing monster.

The policeman took one closer look at the big man, decided he was all right, and returned his papers.

Hatch ran for the departing train and caught the rail of the last car. He jumped, swung on and waved goodbye to the railroad man.

The car was filled far beyond its normal capacity and Hatch was trapped in the crowded corridor. He stood jammed in among a woman with garlic breath, a very young Luftwaffe corporal, and a man in a leather coat, who may have been a salesman or a small shopkeeper, but to the paranoid escapee, he reeked of Gestapo.

A determined porter, carrying a huge suitcase, pushed through the crowd. His forward motion turned Bobby away from the garlic breath and left him pressed against the door of a first class compartment.

His breath clouded the glass, but through the haze he saw a lovely lady draped in a white fox-tail coat. The woman laughed as she accepted a cigarette from a charming Wehrmacht officer beside her. The officer turned as he reached for his lighter, and Bobby's heart froze. The charmer in the gray uniform was Oberstleutnant Strauss!

Hatch sat on the toilet and rocked with the movement of the train. He responded to the third angry rap on the door, hitched up his trousers, and looked into the small cracked mirror over the wash basin. He looked exactly the way he felt. Haggard, hungry, tired, and sick.

"My God," he thought, "if I live through this, I'll write a book. This deserves a book." Then he revised his entire concept. "No, not a book. After this, if I have any brains left at all, I'll forget the whole fucking thing."

Gare d'Austerlitz throbbed with life. Troops, families, hustling porters, police, pretty girls, posters that announced movies, concerts, a Swedish circus, vacations in Spain. Nothing had prepared Hatch for this. The sight stunned him. He was helpless, numbed, and was swept up by the current of the surging crowd. He flowed with it, turned when it turned, and suddenly . . . Paris!

Like any lost tourist, Bobby studied the guide book. It dated back to '32, but when he checked the street sign he was relieved to find that the map was still accurate. He was exactly where he should be and across the wide boulevard was the metro entrance he was looking for.

As he left the underground, he could see three panzer tanks moving down the boulevard Saint-Germain-des-Prés. They flowed with the traffic, stopped when the autos stopped, waited for the gendarme's whistle, then continued along their way. No one else on the boulevard seemed to notice them. After two years of occupation, the tanks were invisible. They were as much a part of the street scene as the pissoirs or the trimmed trees that were beginning to show green.

He walked north along Rue Jacob. There was a nonchalance among the pedestrians, and he desperately hoped he was imitating it. He paused before an art gallery and there, beyond the plate glass, he could see a high ranking SS officer. The man sat comfortably, his legs crossed, a demitasse in his hand. The proprietor rested a landscape on an easel, then stepped to the officer's side and together they shared the pleasure of an old oil that was framed in gold.

Thoughts raced through Hatch's mind. "What's happening here? It's all so damned normal. Am I really going to meet with the Resistance? Is there a Resistance? And if there is, what the hell are they resisting? It's all so normal."

Two blocks down, on the Rue de la Seine, he found what he was looking for: a working class café-bar whose sign was almost completely faded and blended perfectly with the gray building it was in. Just before he entered Chez Victor, he suddenly wished he were in Switzerland!

A tiny bell tinkled as the door closed and Victor looked into the mirror and saw Hatch's reflection. He filled a glass for a customer at the bar and looked at the tall man in the blue suit. The Frenchman was a man of few words and seemed to dare him to order something.

"Un café et un cognac, s'il vous plait," Hatch said.

Victor grunted. He poured the muddy liquid into a cup and slid it to Bobby, then he clanged a small glass down and filled it with brandy. A bit sloshed over the rim, but Victor made no effort to clean it.

"First class," Hatch thought, but said, *"Merci."* He carried the cup and glass to a small table in the rear. He stretched his legs and assumed an imperturbable air as he sized up the area. There was a back door, but he didn't know whether it was locked or where it led. The two guys at the bar seemed innocent enough. Working men, he assumed; but the thug behind the bar, that was another thing. "That's one mean face," Hatch thought. "That guy could blister paint on a wall."

Bobby sipped the cognac, then the coffee, and gagged. "No wonder the son of a bitch is so mean. The slop they served at Gensdorf is better than this. They must make this crap out of old socks." But he smiled and waved his hand for attention.

"Un autre."

The mean man caught his eye and came out from behind the bar with the bottle. Hatch spilt a bit of the cognac, and when Victor approached, he drew a small "v" on the wet table top. The Frenchman took a fraction of a second to read it, then he wiped it dry and grunted.

In his lifetime, Hatch had seen magnificent things. Mountains, lakes that toyed with clouds, majestic seas that assaulted the land with roars and froths of angry white water. But in the moonlight, the blacked out city of Paris was even more beautiful and had more mystery than all of nature.

Bobby had been led through the twisting streets and alleys of the Left Bank. He was told to wait under a street lamp while hidden eyes examined him and double checked his story. Minutes later, a gray Citroen with rusting fenders pulled to the curb and two men with guns pushed him into the rear seat of the car. Hatch's first view of the city was an occasional flash of light that was strong enough to filter through the blindfold that covered his eyes.

Now he was in a tiny room waiting for the men of the FFI to make a decision. He had just settled into a chair when a woman's voice summoned him.

"Captain? Come in, please."

It was a small, well lived in apartment. Books lined the walls and were stacked beside the well-worn, comfortable chairs. There were family photos, a painting of Flemish peasants sowing a field. There were playthings for a child, a lead Eiffel Tower, and a small table with five glasses and an open bottle of wine.

The mean face was smiling at him now. Victor lifted his glass and proposed a toast.

"To victory!"

They touched glasses and chorused, "Victory!" To Hatch's right, André Villon tapped out a foul smelling cigarette. He was in his late thirties, early forties. He was thin, good looking, and tugged at an earlobe when in deep concentration. "Do you know the day of the transport, or how they are going to do it?" he asked.

"No," Hatch said. "I have no idea."

"They're quite capable of bringing them in one at a time, you know." Villon looked to an old man who sat impassively listening to the arguments the men presented.

"It's possible," the old man agreed, "but I think not. Their sense of efficiency would be offended. I think they'll bring them in all at once, but we're still faced with the problem of how to get them out. Half the army will be there to make sure we don't get within a city street of them. It is more than risky; at the moment it seems impossible."

With a wave of her wine glass, Renée called their attention to her. In her simple blouse and skirt, in her thick wooden-soled shoes, she looked like a girl fresh from the farm. Her blond hair encased an innocent face with wide open eyes and a mouth that seemed to counterpoint every sentence she uttered with a slight shy smile. She could and did, when necessary, pass for a teenager; but in fact, Renée was in her thirties, a widow, a nonpracticing lawyer, and one of the leaders of the Resistance.

"It is too early," she said, looking directly at Hatch, "for us in any way to consider this plan. There are too many negatives. If we try and take them off the train, there will be too many dead.

That is for sure. We have tried it before and we have failed. If we try and take them here in Paris, there will be a battle in the streets, and we cannot win against tanks and machine guns."

"I agree," said Bobby. "Look, lady, you don't have to convince me. It's the colonel who thinks . . ."

André interrupted him. He was defensive, and the ear tugging became obsessive. "I know what your colonel thinks, but he has been a prisoner for a long time. He has no contact with reality."

Hatch wanted to agree, but instead said, "Maybe; but I got out of prison, and they said it was impossible."

Renée got to her feet and there was a trace of annoyance in her voice. "One man is not a football team that is coming to occupied France to play against the Nazis. I tell you, when they get to Colombe Stadium, the Boche will have at least a battalion in front of the place."

"I agree," Bobby said with a wave of his hands. "Look, I'm just a pilgrim on my way to a shrine in Switzerland. It's not my idea."

"Just a moment," the old man interrupted. "I didn't know they were to play at the Colombe Stadium." There was an excitement in his voice. "Why didn't anyone say that before?" All eyes turned to him. "There are, as you know, 300 miles of tunnels under our city. And I know them like the back of my hand. When the stadium was built, we had to reinforce its foundations so that it would not fall through into the sewers."

"Are you sure?" Renée asked.

"But of course. I worked there for thirty years. I was chief engineer for almost fifteen years."

The room was silent for a moment. Somewhere beyond the lawns of the Tuilleries, a tank rumbled. In an apartment close by, a child cried.

André tugged at his ear. *"Ça change tout!"* he said. "That changes everything!"

"Not yet!" Renee's tone was sharp, almost shrill. "First we have a look."

There was an anger about the woman that disturbed Bobby. He knew it wasn't directed at him, but he took it personally and shifted uncomfortably in his seat.

She turned her eyes to the old man. "Claude, can you get into the tunnels?"

"Yes. There are Germans down there, but not many."

"Good," she said. "Do it soon." There was dismissal in her tone, and the men got to their feet.

"This house is safe," André said to Hatch. "You will stay here with Renée. Okay?"

"Suits me fine," Bobby said.

When the men left, Renée went directly to the kitchen.

"I'm sorry," she said as she placed a large pan on the stove. "I know that you must be famished, but we had to talk."

"I understand," Bobby said. He walked into the small room and watched her closely as she trimmed some vegetables and diced a small piece of meat. It had been many years since he had last seen a woman fuss about her kitchen. There was nothing sexual about any of her movements, yet Bobby was overcome with the sensuality of her. She sensed his eyes, turned, and stared coldly at him before she returned to the cutting board.

"Look," Hatch said, "I just want to talk. It's been a long time since I talked to a woman."

She placed the pan on the stove and adjusted the fire. "I understand."

"Then why don't we sit down? Bobby—my friends call me Bobby."

She turned to him and chose her words very carefully. "I didn't want to hear your name, and now that I have, I don't want to hear anything else about you. The less I know, the better it is for you."

"And for you?"

"Yes," she said softly, "and for me too."

She brushed passed him and stopped at the wine. "Would you like some?"

"Yes, please."

She filled both glasses and they sat listening to the dim sounds of the city.

"I'm sorry," Hatch said, feeling drowsy. He realized he hadn't had any sleep in more than 48 hours. "My being here has put you and your friends in a tough spot. I'm truly sorry."

Renée carefully sipped at the wine. "Being in a tough spot, as you call it, is where I choose to be. There are thousands of us out there. Communists, anarchists, but all French, all choosing to be in this tough spot."

"Then why do you seem so angry? What have I done?"

"You?" she said, sounding a bit astounded. "You have done nothing. It is the war, and if I appear angry, it is not at you. When I hear that someone I sheltered is safe, I am happy. I can forget them. But when I hear that someone has been caught or killed, then I remember everything. Their faces, their voices, what they said about their families. Their children, even their pets." Her open eyes looked directly into his. "I mourn for them. I don't want to mourn for you."

"You don't have to worry about me," Hatch said, trying to break the mood.

"No?"

"No, not a bit. First of all, I'm an orphan. I have no family, no friends, no children. I never even had a pet . . . so there," he smiled, "Nothing to worry about, nothing to remember."

Renée bent to fill his glass. When she looked up again, he was asleep, his head resting on his shoulder, his face relaxed as if he hadn't a trouble in the world. She removed his shoes, covered him with a blanket, and he slept ten hours into the morning.

Von Steiner felt grand. It was the first truly beautiful day of spring, and as his open-topped car sped along Unter den Linden towards the Brandenberg Gate, his mind was clear. Everything seemed to be going well. The reports from Hoppy Muller and Helmut were glowing, and every word from Gensdorf told him that Colby had his men under control and a team worthy of playing against the German Nationals was actually being formed.

This was the first time Kurt had ever been summoned to party headquarters, and he thought he knew why. Although he had not seen Herr Lorenz since that evening meeting in General Lang's office, he had heard that Lorenz had been promoted and was now a close confidant of the Führer. He knew that the party man's invisible hand had made the uniforms and equipment possible and that the preparations for the game at Colombe Stadium was under his direct supervision.

Kurt sat back, pulled his kid leather gloves tight, and drew a deep, relaxing breath. He had just received a commendation, and he somehow suspected that Lorenz had a hand in that, too. He leaned forward and touched the shoulder of his driver.

"Max," he said, "slow down. We have some time and it is a beautiful day."

The film skipped a frame and blinked black as the American landing craft hit the rocky Italian beach at Anzio. Battle hardened troops poured out of the beached monsters and rushed headlong into bursts of machine gun and artillery fire. An armada, guns blazing, held the horizon. Under the sound of music and battle, a strident narrator described the action.

"The combined forces of England, France, and America have succeeded in breaching the first walls of fortress Europe."

An American fighter plane's erratic camera caught tracer bullets as they tore into a German convoy, the helpless troops scattering amid fire and explosions. The scene cut to GIs attacking a bunker. One, hit, fell; a comrade tossed a grenade; and the German defenders ran forward, one on fire, the other, broken, fell doll-like amid the debris.

"The heavily entrenched German forces, feeling the bite of the Allied effort, retreat before the victorious attackers."

The music became dramatic as the camera focused on long lines of bedraggled German prisoners. British Tommies, armed with the latest automatic weapons, guarded the defeated men.

With the cut, the music became martial. Squadrons of Spitfires peeled off out of formation, attacking a target below them.

"The sky is ours, and to quote an old warrior, 'We have met the enemy, and he is ours.' "

Lorenz spoke into the microphone beside him, the screen ground to darkness, the lights rose in the projection room and Kurt sat in silence staring at the white beaded screen. Lorenz's voice came from the rear of the room. "Remind you of something, Von Steiner?"

"Yes, Herr Lorenz, it does."

The man's voice dropped. "And what does it remind you of, Major?"

Kurt rose to his feet and faced the man. "It reminds me of our own films, Herr Lorenz. Poland, France, Belgium . . ."

"Et cetera, et cetera, et cetera."

There was accusation in the man's voice, and Kurt felt as if he were in a sickening free fall where nothing but gravity was master.

"I don't understand, Herr Lorenz. I have just received a commendation from the Führer himself complimenting my department for its initiative."

The Nazi spoke as he reached for a cigar. "Yes, of course, Major. The Führer is very pleased, particularly with our scheme." He rolled the cigar between his fingers. "But as you can see, the news is not good. The Führer must remain pleased, the people must be reassured, and our team must win. At all costs we must retain control of the situation."

"But, Herr Lorenz," Kurt protested, "I don't understand. We are in control. Under the circumstances, I think we are very much in control."

"Then how did one of the players manage to escape such fine control, Major?"

Kurt was visibly shaken at the words, and Lorenz was surprised at the reaction.

"You didn't know?"

He shook his head dumbly. "Who?"

"The American." He took a quick glance at a dossier before him. "Robert Hatch, a captain." He stared at Kurt, and his voice softened. "Sit down, Major. This is serious business and I think we ought to discuss it."

Lorenz had thought his idea through and if Kurt concurred, he would implement it.

"This escape must never happen again. There are too many eyes to see it, it casts too much doubt upon our efficiency. My plan is simple." He pulled another file. "This Captain Colby. He was there at the beginning, was he not?"

"Yes, he was."

"Perfect." The Nazi grinned. "Perfect. I suggest we make an example of him. If we shoot their captain and leader, I don't think another escape will be, how shall we say, Major, in the cards?"

Kurt was suddenly on his feet. In the dark overheated screening room, his hands were cold, he felt a tremor running through his body.

"That's impossible, sir. Completely out of the question. Colby is not only the backbone of the team, he is the playmaker, the center that makes them a team. If we kill him, there will be a very little to show the world, very little to please our Führer. That is impossible." Kurt snapped to attention and held tightly to Lorenz's eyes. "I will be fully responsible for the Allied players. If such a thing should happen again, I, sir, will present myself to you personally, and you may do with me as you wish."

Lorenz laughed. He laughed hard, tears came to his eyes. "You know, I like you, Major," he said. "I like you very much. But you have no concept of political reality. I don't want your head, but I don't want mine to roll either. You see, the game is no longer yours alone. It is ours, and we have a shared responsibility. So if you assure me that this will not happen again, I accept your word; because if it does, we will both be visited in the night. And believe me, if that should happen, we will never get to see the game at Colombe Stadium."

In the past months, "responsibility" had become the key word in most military conversations. Everyone talked of it, shunned it, passed it on to someone else. Von Steiner used the magic word to soothe the fears and anger of both the Kommandant and his immediate superiors. When he heard the fall of the guard's boots, he swung his injured leg off the Kommandant's desk and made himself ready for Colby.

John knew Willinger would come down hard, but he never expected so strong a reaction. All team play was suspended and the men restricted to the hut. Anton and Hans were transferred, and the new goons were front line troops—edgy, suspicious, and unused to the closed in spaces of a prison.

"Of course," Kurt said, "the team will resume its training immediately. I've already cleared this with Kommandant Willinger. But you must give me your word that this will never happen again."

Colby was uncomfortable; he had had many encounters with the Major before, but he had never seen him angry or, as he perceived, frightened.

"Hatch's escape had nothing to do with the team. That was his own idea."

"But the men covered for him."

Colby took the offensive. "Of course they did. What would you expect them to do? What would you do under the same circumstances?"

Kurt had thought of this. As a soldier, he knew it was a prisoner's right, his duty, to escape if the opportunity presented itself.

"I want your word, Captain."

John shook his head slowly. There was almost a sadness in his voice. "I can't give it to you. I'm sorry."

Kurt walked to the door. "I'm sorry too." He paused with his hand on the knob. "You will continue the practice sessions, but you will be guarded, closely guarded, by men who have orders to shoot."

Kurt called the guards, and Colby was marched between them back to the compound.

CHAPTER THIRTEEN

The Germans were everywhere. In groups of twos and threes, massed on buses, generally on their best behavior, and always with cameras. Paris was their captured jewel, the prize of prizes, and it was important for them to be seen back home—in Baden-Baden, or Hamburg, or Frankfurt am Main—with the Eiffel Tower or the Louvre or Notre Dame. Like hunters posing with a dead lion or rhino, the soldiers wanted photographs of themselves and the kill.

When the sanitation truck pulled up before the Café Monaco and the workmen in "bleu de travail," their traditional work clothes, leapt down, the sight of them touched an esthetic nerve in Luftwaffe Sergeant Mayer. He approached an irresistible old man with a hand-rolled cigarette in his mouth and an eye partially hidden by a pulled down beret.

"Pardonez-moi," Mayer said, using a phrase borrowed from his tourist dictionary. *"Photo?"*

"Oui," the old man said, *"c'est bien."*

The sergeant moved to his side and called to his friend Krueger, who adjusted his 35mm Leica.

Mayer smiled, Victor struck a pose, and Krueger took the shot.

"Merci, merci," The Luftwaffe man said and grinned triumphantly back to his table and comrade.

The Frenchmen went on with their work. They pried the manhole cover up and disappeared down into the bowels of the city.

Across from the Café Monaco, across a narrow stretch of lawn, behind rows of blooming tulips, the gray walls of Colombe Stadium reached forty feet into the sky and curved off toward the Seine. Renée measured the distance with her eye, waited until the last of the men disappeared, then she finished her aperitif, left enough francs, and wandered down the narrow street.

"Mademoiselle!" Mayer called and waved the Leica. "Photo?"

Renée turned, and the look in her eye left the German with the very clear impression that not everyone in Paris liked him.

Bobby lit a cigarette, took a drag, and stamped it out immediately. The smoke tore at his throat and the coughing brought tears to his eyes. He tore the butt open and fingered the corn silk that was wrapped in thick paper, then shook his head in wonder. Nothing was real, not the coffee or the leather. Silk stockings were painted onto smoothly shaved legs. Even the gas that drove the few civilian vehicles was a mixture of gasoline and something invented. Paris had become a strange world of the ersatz, where only the black market and the German street signs and memories were real.

Renée entered the apartment so silently, he was startled when he saw her.

"Hello." He waved. "How's it going?"

She sank wearily into a chair, lit one of the cornsilk cigarettes, and inhaled deeply.

"We will know this evening. If we are lucky, the old man will be wrong, if not . . ." if not," she repeated, "we will have a big, big problem on our hands."

Bobby sat in the chair opposite hers and leaned forward.

"I know you don't want to know anything about me, and I understand that, but is there anything in the book about you? I mean, my knowing anything about you?"

When she didn't answer, he persisted with a smile. "After all," he said, "we are sort of roommates."

"Roommates?" She answered his smile. "That is such an American expression. I was an au pair in Greenwich, Connecticut. I lived with an American family." She laughed a small laugh as she remembered. "It seems so long ago."

"I lived near Greenwich." He was eager now, he wanted desperately to talk. "I lived in New York City. Then I went to school in the Midwest. I'm an engineer."

Her face fell, for a moment her protective veil dropped, but she quickly recovered. "My husband was an engineer." She paused. "He was killed in North Africa, almost a year ago."

"I'm sorry."

"It is done." She shrugged. "It is a reality, and we must lean to live with realities. I have a son, François. He is named after his father. He is a wonderful boy."

"Where is he now?"

"With my mother. This is a safe house, but he is safer with my mother. If the Boche should come here they will not see that he is only six years old. They will only see a French thing, and they will kill him, or send him to Ravensbruck and kill him there." She fell silent for a moment. "The Boche, they are truly pigs. It would be nice if your football team could beat them, beat them badly." She looked directly at him. "Can they beat them? Can they beat the Germans?"

"I don't know," Hatch said. "I know they want to, but I don't know."

They sat circling the map whose edges were held down by short stacks of books. The old man traced the twists of the tunnel that fed into the river then traced back to their point of entry at the Café Monaco.

"The foundation of the stadium is exactly where I remembered it to be. Of course, we will have to get hold of the original plans, but I think we can tunnel directly up into the visitor's changing room."

"Yeah," Hatch agreed, "they'll probably be left alone at half time. You could do it then."

"Oui," the old man said. "That is what we intended. Through the floor and roof, into the underground. We will then dynamite the entrance. With all the twists and turns, it might be an hour or more before they find the route we've taken."

"What about the way out? There must be more than one way out," Renée said. "As soon as the swine find out that the players are gone, they will be everywhere."

"Yes, that is true," André said. "But if you follow the map," he kneeled and retraced the route they had taken that afternoon, "you will see that here, here, here, and here," he pointed to sewer exits at the four points, "we can, with some planning, have autos waiting; and if that is barred, we take to the catacombs and feed directly out into the Seine." He paused. "That, in my opinion, is perhaps the best way to go. We can have a barge with river clearance waiting that can take them as far as the Spanish border. The Maquis can handle it there."

Renée paced, then she stopped, looked at Hatch and smiled. "We are unlucky. This looks as if it can work."

André pushed the books from the outer edges of the map, rolled it, and slipped it into a cardboard cylinder.

"We will begin preparation immediately. There is much to do. The automobiles, perhaps some German uniforms, contact with the Maquis." He tugged at his ear then lit one of the corn silk cigarettes. "When you return to the camp, you will tell your colonel exactly what our plan is. The men must be prepared."

Hatch felt as if something was trying to claw through his stomach and escape through his navel. "Return to what!?"

"To the camp, of course." Then he saw Hatch's face and felt his pain. "I'm sorry," he said quietly, 'but there is no other way. I thought you understood that. How else will they know that we have a plan or what the plan is, if you do not return?"

Hatch sat stunned, his head shook in disbelief. "That fucking Waldron," he murmured under his breath.

"What?" the nervous Frenchman asked.

"It took me a year to get out of there," he said to no one in particular. Then anger replaced shock. "What the hell am I supposed to do, bust back into the camp? Rip off all my clothes and yell, 'Hey, fellas, look at me, bare ass Bobby Hatch is back!' " He fell back defeated. "How the hell do I do it?"

They waited until his anger had subsided; then, after a nod from Renée, the old man cleared his throat and spoke. "You get captured."

"Get captured?" Bobby roared, knowing he was fighting a useless fight. "Yeah, suppose I get captured and they send me to the wrong place? What about that?"

The old man shook his head. "No. The Boche will take you to the same place again to show the other prisoners that you are not a success."

"All the answers. You got all the fucking answers, don't you?"

He slumped into his seat, and Renée filled his wine glass to the brim.

Bobby lay back gnawing at his bitterness. Never in his endless nights as a prisoner had he dreamt that a small bit of freedom could taste so sweet. Pictures reeled through his mind. The night run through the forest, the train, the shock of seeing Strauss, the railway station, the crowds, the metro, the boulevards. The evening alone with Renée, the smell of her, the marvelous movements of her body, the taste of wine. He closed his eyes tightly trying to lock the memories in, and when he opened them, she was there.

She took hours preparing herself for this occasion. She chilled the long hidden bottle of champagne, and from beneath the Belgian lace that was part of her dowry, she removed and unfolded silken mysteries. Panties and matching bra that, in the semi-darkness of the moonlit room, would transform themselves to magic. For the first time in years she wore real stockings. She leaned back and rolled them slowly over her calves, her knees, her thighs, the black silk caressing the soft flesh that yielded to the clips of the garter belt. She brushed her hair until it crackled. She touched her ears, the tips of her shoulders, the two secret places beneath her breasts with tiny dabs of perfume; she slipped into the Hanoi robe, the one with the wild jungle bird embroidered on the back, the one she knew he loved so much.

"*François, je t'aime, mon amour*. I love you, and I've missed you very much."

She killed the lights in the room and lit candles. Through her tears, the lights seemed like faceted jewels. This evening she would welcome her husband back from his long war, soothe his warrior's body, soothe his soul. Then she would say goodbye to him forever and keep only the memory of his eyes and the way he laughed locked deeply within her heart.

CHAPTER FOURTEEN

"If they're gonna take me, I'll be god damned if I'm gonna run into their arms. Let 'em take me off the streets."

And they did. But before that, he saw the city. He walked along the Seine, crossed the Pont de Puteaux to the magnificent lawns and houses of the Bois de Boulogne. He audaciously flirted with two lady German soldiers, whom the Parisians called "souris grises," gray mice. He saw the outside of the Louvre, recrossed the river at Pont Neuf, walked the Boulevard Saint Michel, and had a drink at Deux Magots. Slightly drunk, he was picked up an hour after curfew, interrogated, and sent back to Gensdorf.

Because Kommandant Willinger was not the brightest of men, he ordered the entire prisoner population out of their huts to watch the return of the escapee. Bobby Hatch was delivered caged in the back of an army truck and, thirty seconds after his arrival, was a hero-celebrity.

The goons pushed him through the ranks towards the solitary confinement cells; and from all outward appearances, he seemed chipper, almost glad to be "home." He waved to Colby.

"Hey, what do you say, Johnny? How are your babies doing?"

The guards pushed him again. He caught Major Rose's eye and nodded a definite "yes," then shouted, "Hey, Rosie, regards from the outside. Have I got things to tell you!"

This time he was knocked to the ground, and the prisoners almost broke ranks, but the dogs and the angry look of the guards kept them in line.

McFarlin, the redhead from Belfast, began to chant, and hundreds of voices joined him. "Hatch! Hatch! Hatch!"

The sound cheered Bobby for a while, then in total misery he curled into a small ball and, in the darkness of the cell, fell into a deep sleep.

Colby sat as far back in the chair as he could. The room around him seemed to have shifted. He looked to the ceiling of the colonel's quarters, then brought his eyes back to the men of the committee.

"I don't believe it. This time I believe you've all gone completely bonkers. Not only are you going to get all the men on my squad killed, but you've involved innocent Frenchmen. How in the world are you going to pull this off?"

Rose nervously cleared his throat. "We're not quite sure, as a matter of fact. You know as much about it as we do, and that is that an escape has been planned and is presently being prepared by the Resistance. The answer to all our questions is with Hatch."

"The poor son of a bitch," Colby said and thumped the table. "To have gotten as far as Paris and then to have turned around and walked into the cooler is more than I can understand. It's either the bravest or the stupidest act I've ever heard of."

"We like to think him a brave man, Colby," the colonel said with a hard cutting edge. "I know it's difficult for you to grasp, but try."

"All right, I'll buy that. I happen to like that idiot, you know. What I don't like is the image of him spending three or four months sleeping on a concrete floor and eating bread soaked in water." A stillness filled the room. For a minute each man was alone with his thoughts. "All right," Colby continued, "supposing my men were crazy enough to go along with this suicide pact of yours. How do we get the hero out of the cooler so he can tell us exactly how we're going to get killed?"

Waldron brushed his hair back with his hands. "We thought you would talk to your friend Von Steiner. Hatch is officially your trainer, and as such, that might get him out."

John shook his head. "No. He'll never buy that. You'll have to think of something else." He got to his feet. "I've got a training session to go to, gentlemen." Then he glared at Waldron. "I'd like to leave you with a thought, Colonel. If you ever refer to Von Steiner as my friend again, I will break your fucking nose. And that, sir, is a promise."

He stood trembling, his fists clenched, his knuckles white, and there was no doubt in any of the nervous men that he meant every word.

Seconds after the door closed behind the furious Welshman, Sherlock said, "I think you're right, Colonel. I think the man should be shot."

Colby watched the team working the pitch. It was a week to game time, he knew they would never be better, and he took a mental inventory of just what they had going for them.

Peiter van Beck, whose legs were not fully healed, whose every movement, every kick was a triumph of the will.

Jean-Paul Remy, nervous, high strung, unpredictable, probably working towards a breakdown.

Gunner Nilsson, a good man but young, untried. Helmut Rheingold's men would probably eat him alive.

Fernandez, a fucking genius.

Tony Morell, not the best, but a hard-working professional, and better than competent goalkeeper.

Carlos Rey, fast, a good team man.

Sid Harman, solid as a rock. The only man really capable of a full ninety minutes of play.

Again and again he ran them through his mind. He added, he saw them work, he subtracted. "My God," he said, "My good God, we've got a chance. With a little luck, just a little, we can win!"

That evening he told them the reason Hatch had come back, then he put the vote to the team. The result was two to one in favor of escape.

CHAPTER FIFTEEN

At the moment, Waldron could think of nothing in the world he despised more than the two men that shared the room with him. He stood at parade rest, his chest out, jaws clenched, hands locked tightly behind him. He was determined not to give an inch.

"Along with other senior officers who will represent their various countries, you, Colonel Waldron, and your aides, Major Rose and Captain Sherlock, will travel to Paris."

"I won't do it."

"You have no choice," Von Steiner said.

"Then I'll travel," Waldron growled, "but I'll be damned if I'll represent anything."

Kurt shrugged. "As you like, Colonel." Then he turned to Colby. "You, Captain, will have your team ready to travel on Thursday. If there are any changes, I will inform you as soon as possible. Are there any questions, gentlemen?"

John tried to hide the anxiety in his voice by assuming an air of complete nonchalance. "One of my key men is in the punishment block, in solitary. I need him and I'd like you to get him out if you can."

"Impossible!" Von Steiner shouted. Then in a gesture of total exasperation, he slapped his hands against his thighs. "He was not caught stealing a bowl of strawberries, you know. He endangered this entire effort, as well as our lives, with his stupid attempt at escape. It is impossible. If you need another trainer, I'll get you one, but not the American."

"He's not my trainer anymore," Colby said, "he's my goalkeeper."

"Tony Morell is your goalkeeper," Von Steiner shot back.

"Not any more. He's broken his arm."

Waldron lifted his brows imperceptibly, and Kurt stared at the Welshman. "When did this happen?"

"This morning during practice."

Von Steiner shook his head violently. "Impossible. Put someone else in goal."

"Who?" Colby asked quickly. "You know the squad as well as I, you've seen them play. Who can fill that position at this late date? You want us packed and on the train by Thursday, who can I train and put into that position?"

Von Steiner shook his head in disbelief. He took only a moment to answer, knowing there could be no game that would have any meaning if the position wasn't properly filled. "If our camp doctor verifies the broken arm, you may have the

American. But if he attempts another escape, I will order him shot on the spot, and one of our men will fill the position in front of your net. Is that understood, Captain?"

The two British officers were marched back to the prisoners' side of the camp by SS guards, and as soon as they were delivered and alone, the colonel turned to Colby.

"Is it possible that we have you all wrong, Captain?"

"No, sir, it's not. We both know exactly who and what we are. I suppose in our own ways, we're both fearsome sons of bitches." He snapped a salute. "Excuse me, sir, but I have things to do."

That afternoon Waldron gave the command. Colby was to have anything he wanted and the total cooperation of every man.

"Listen to me," Tony Morell said. "There are a few things I want to make very clear. First of all, I don't particularly like the Yank. He's a bit of a pain in the arse, you know, and his hoppin' about makes me nervous. The second thing is, I'm against the escape. I think it's dangerous and stupid. I want to play against Jerry and I think we've got a chance."

He lit one of the Red Cross "Luckies" and sat down beside John.

"And the third reason, which is not the last, nor the least, is that I don't particularly relish the idea of getting my bloody arm broken." He looked at Colby. "Ya didn't say which arm, did ya?"

John shook his head and whispered, "No."

"Then make it the left, and make it a clean break." Tony forced a laugh which made him look even more miserable. "I won't even get to see the game, will I?"

John desperately wanted to say something to compensate this marvelous and brave man, but he couldn't at first find the words.

"One of the first, and perhaps the only good thing I ever learned in the service of His Majesty the King," he finally said, "was never leave your wounded. The only way I'd leave you, Tony, is if they shot me, and I don't think the bastards'll do that until after the game."

Fernandez and Terry Brad held the goalkeeper's arm tightly between them, exposing only the area between the elbow and shoulder. Sweat ran down Doug Clure's temples. He looked at Tony, the man nodded, Clure took aim and kicked.

That afternoon the German x-ray showed the slightest of breaks along the humerus. In a month the arm would be completely healed.

It took two full days for Bobby to work "solitary" out of his limbs, then the team took him in hand. They fired balls at him from all directions and stopped only when his hands began to swell.

Bobby lay back on his bunk and rubbed his palms with alcohol. "You crazy bastards. What are you trying to do, kill me?"

"We only have half a game," John said. "And I want it to be the best half any team ever played." Then he changed his tone. "How was it?" he asked hungrily. "Was it beautiful?"

"Yeah," Hatch said, and his mind sped back to his few moments of freedom.

"Tell me," Colby said. "Did you have a woman? Did you get drunk? Did you see much of the city?"

"I had it all, Johnny boy, I had it all."

"Well then, tell me. Don't just sit there, you twit. Tell me all."

"It was everything I imagined it would be," Hatch said, "and more."

John leaned forward, his face serious, his mind focused, intent on Bobby's story.

"As soon as I walked into Chez Victor I knew that there was something right about the joint. Candles, mirrors, a small jazz band playing in the back. Then this knockout broad in a black, way off the shoulder dress, walks up to me. I give her the secret handshake and I can feel the lights go on in her head, and I know right off, she's mine if I want her." He lapsed into a deep dream-like state. Then, with a voice that grated with impatience, Colby said, "Damn it, man, go on. What happened then?"

"Then?" Bobby asked, pulling himself back to the present. "Oh yeah, then. Then we slipped out the back door and took some of those winding streets to her place near the river. It had a fully stocked bar, and while I'm mixing a drink she disappears on me. I sit down in one of those big overstuffed chairs and snap on the radio. I'm tired, see, so I doze off for, I don't know, a half hour maybe. Then I feel these fingers on my cheeks. I open my eyes and there she is in one of those red see-through nightgowns. 'Cherie,' she says, 'I have not yet called the Resistance. First, we save ourselves, then we save France.' "

John looked at him and said gravely, "You're lying, you bastard!"

"Yeah," he said with a maddening grin, "I'm lying!"

Colby flung a football at him and the American headed it back.

A platoon of Wehrmacht, fully officered and armed for what seemed like combat, surrounded the single coach that stood waiting at a siding near the main line. When the bus arrived, half the platoon, moving on command, broke ranks. Some surrounded the vehicle, others with rifles ready formed a double line that led from the bus to the coach. The players stepped off and walked through the phalanx of guns. Some laughed, some were somber, but they all felt the furies of the game.

It was first class, but there were bars welded to the sealed windows and the guards beyond the doors looked ready for any possible trouble. They crossed the frontier just as the sun broke the horizon. Silhouettes of men began to appear, and the new sun stained the earth of the plowed fields red.

Hatch stared at the passing panorama and wondered where he had seen it before. He thought of it and remembered the Flemish painting of farmers seeding, and for a fleeting moment his mind flashed to Renée and their few hours of shared humanity and warmth.

Jean-Paul Remy rocked with the rhythm of the train. This was La Belle France, and everything he remembered in his young life seemed to flash before him as they raced before the sun. He thought he saw a lady high on a hill beside an old oak. "Mamma," he said softly, almost inaudibly, "Mamma."

They passed a church, ran through a stand of poplars; the sun was up now and glared into his eyes. He got to his feet and began to pace the narrow aisle of the compartment. Michel thought of stopping him, talking to him, then thought it best to leave him alone with his memories.

"Hey, Tony," Hatch said, and the goalkeeper turned to him. "How's the arm?"

"All right, I guess."

"All right means you'll be able to lift a glass pretty soon. First drinks in London are on me." Then a troubled look came into his eyes. "Hey, Tony, tell me something. Where do I stand for a corner kick?"

"What?"

"I keep blocking it out. I mean I'm going through all the plays in my head, and I'm drawing a blank on this one."

Morell stared at him until his despair gave way to amusement, and he laughed. "Go to sleep, Hatch. It'll do us both a great deal of good." He laughed again, then closed his eyes and pretended to sleep.

Remy rapped on the glass and the guard turned and looked at him impassively. *"Toilette?"* He shouted over the clatter of the wheels. *"Toilette?"*

The soldier signaled him to wait then returned with a captain, who drew his sidearm. He opened the door and Jean-Paul stepped into the corridor. His nervousness and quiet mumblings disturbed Michel. He watched him as long as he could, then he put his uneasiness aside and was lost in the fantasy of escape and his first taste of freedom.

The guard at the lavatory came to attention at the sight of the officer and player. Remy paused before the door, the captain stepped aside, then in one quick motion the Frenchman clamped an arm around the officer's neck and pulled the Luger from his hand. The gun looked large in the hands of the soccer player. His eyes were wild and the guard froze as Remy backed into the lavatory, hauling the gasping captain with him. As soon as the door closed, the guard gave the alarm. In seconds the train braked, and everyone and everything jolted forward.

Jean-Paul's head shattered the toilet's mirror. The sudden pain and loss of gravity pulled his body stiff, and he touched the trigger and blew the German's face away. He smashed the Luger through the window then kicked out the remaining glass.

The players watched the scene in disbelief. It seemed like a film unreeling or a strange slow motion dream. Jean-Paul plunging down an embankment then up into a surrounding wheat field. Soldiers massing and firing, the sound of bullets mute within the confines of the train. Jean-Paul running, little puffs of grain and earth exploding around him. Now Remy the athlete loped across the golden field, first to his right, then straight, then to the left. He was perfect. He seemed to time the bullets, time the shift of the rifles. A hill loomed before him, a small mound of earth that would shelter him from the hail of lead. He ran victorious to its apex, he looked black against the silver morning sky; then, like a marionette ending a performance for children, he threw his hands high into the air and fell.

CHAPTER SIXTEEN

They came in buses and trucks, jammed into autos, into special trains. They carried hampers of food and beer and wine; and because admission was free, the queues started forming days before, and special police were assigned to keep order. It was more than just a game—it was combat, and all of Paris, all of the world knew it.

The stadium walls were lined with flags that fluttered in the early morning breeze, and the whipping motion of the red and black banners counterpointed the blare of the many military bands that welcomed the crowds and select groups of the Wehrmacht, the Luftwaffe, submarine heroes, and the SS.

By direct order from the Führer himself, the event was a state occasion, and every breast gleamed with medals and iron crosses dangled from the necks of heroes.

Under the old man's supervision, the diggers drew power from the same source that lit the stadium. The throw of light masked the half dozen men with grotesque shadows of noses, ears, hats. The tunnel echoed with the sound of picks and the grunts of men passing the earth and dislodged rocks that were dumped into the surging, stinking sewer that fed out into the beautiful Seine.

Herr Lorenz, in a new Bavarian hat complete with feather and crest, inspected the visitor's changing room. A nervous security man stood at his side.

"We will need soldiers outside the door and beneath both windows," he barked.

"Jawohl, Herr Lorenz." He jotted the sacred command down on a large lineless pad.

"Unless the situation is completely out of hand, there is to be no bloodshed. I want a complete team out on that field today. Is that understood?"

"Jawohl." The security man nodded. "It will be just as you say, Herr Lorenz."

The hooded trucks slowly eased their way through the mass of people. The soldier drivers who were guaranteed tickets felt festive. They gleefully beeped their horns and flirted with the "mademoiselles" who were dressed for summer.

The guards at the wall swung the great gates open and the vehicles entered the dark underground of the stadium. The canvas flap was pulled back, the team leapt onto the concrete floor and faced a squad of SS, their automatic weapons pointed directly at them.

"So this is it. This is the payoff," Sid Harmer

thought. "It's almost ending the way it began—with the fuckers in front of us with guns." He felt a sudden rush of anger as the word "ending" repeated itself in his mind. He wanted to play the game out, he wanted to beat the bastards. He looked at his teammates and wondered how many of them felt the way he did. He turned and caught the eye of the West Indian, who was grinning.

"Look at them," Fernandez said with the Calypso lilt Harmer had learned to love. "Oh, how they'd love to shoot us, but they can't, at least not until after the first half." Then he shouted, "Kiss my black arse!"

And Sid waved a single stiff finger that showed his solidarity with the man from the Caribbean.

From somewhere above them a band struck up a march, and thousands cheered.

The SS officer called them to attention. The men fell into line and started forward to the stairwell that would lead them to the changing room. The rhythm of the marching men and guards blended with the beat of the band. On command, they paused before a steel door that was racked back with a roar of bearings. The officer released them, and they broke formation and ran shouting to the door assigned to them.

"How interesting," Colby thought. It was strikingly like the beginning of any other game played. The music, the sound of the gathering crowd, the men tense, psyching themselves for the task ahead. It was all the same, only the stakes were higher.

Then he too began to run and shout. He was caught in the energy and followed the team into the visitor's changing room.

Von Steiner sat in the dugout and watched the stadium fill. The French swarmed whistling and catcalling into the stands, and he knew they would be wild at game time, possibly out of hand, and he wondered about the security. The band struck a new tune, lines of soldiers slipped into the seats reserved for them, and Kurt grinned. The stands were filled, the stadium began to breathe like a living thing, and he realized that his impossible event was indeed a reality.

John moved among the men. In their flaming red uniforms, the "Cardinals of Gensdorf" looked magnificent to him. He stopped beside Arthur Hayes and pulled the rear of his jersey down.

"Are you all right, Arthur?"

"I'm a bit stiff."

He affectionately rapped the player's shoulder. "You'll be fine when you're a bit warmer."

Sid called, "John, do you want me back for corners?"

"Yeah, absolutely."

He walked to Hatch. "How are you doing?"

Bobby's eyes were narrowed with worry. "Colby . . ." His voice trailed off and he looked down at his blue goalkeeper's shirt.

"Yes, what is it?"

"I—" then he blurted, "where do I stand for a corner kick?"

John was staggered. "Are you serious?"

"Please." The large eyes begged.

Colby shook his head in disbelief. "May God have mercy on us." Then he smiled at the absurdity of it all. "The far post," he said. "The far post facing the ball."

The large eyes were grateful and the voice sincere. "Thanks, buddy. Thanks a million."

"It's okay," Colby said, then pulled his red jersey over his head and smiled.

Every man was readying himself for the battle. Even Hatch had the taste of the game in his mouth, and not one of them mentioned half time and the escape.

At mid-field, just behind the dugout area, the roped off seats were beginning to fill.

Generaloberst Alfred Jodl, the chief of the general staff, arrived with a woman of striking beauty whose long hair was piled high and bound in braids. In minutes, Jodl was joined by the military commander of greater Paris, whose guest was Pierre Laval, the head of the Vichy government.

Motion picture cameras under the supervision of a vivacious blond lady were placed throughout the arena. The Führer had sent her to document every aspect of the event. She had three cameras photograph the arrival of the Allied officers.

Waldron glared into the camera's eye. If he was to be a participant in the motion picture, then he wanted Herr Hitler to see the face of contempt. The soldiers around the British officers represented the defeated continent; they were totally aware of the gravity and uniqueness of the event and sat straight and silent. The shabbiness of their prison-worn uniforms somehow added dignity to their appearance.

Otto Boehm chatted into a microphone in perfect BBC English. Beside him, his colleagues, fluent in several languages, broadcast out into the world. Boehm sipped some water and cleared his throat.

"And so, a hearty welcome to all our listeners in England. There are just a few minutes to go before the kickoff of this historic match. Just below our microphones there are French and Germans shaking hands. In this great crowd of 50,000, I can see General De Renesse for France and Colonel Cedric Waldron representing Great Britain."

A sergeant handed the broadcaster a note. He accepted it with a nod, read it at a glance, and announced, "To insure fair play and good sportsmanship, the German organizers have picked Karl Vogel, a Swiss, to referee the match."

Kurt slipped into his seat between Lorenz and General Lang. Four blond boys in the black lederhosen of the Hitler Youth dashed onto the field and placed the corner flags around the pitch. The small pennants were black and red with a swastika circled in the center. There were a few catcalls from the stands.

Lorenz stiffened and turned to Kurt. "We will win, won't we, Major?"

"I think so," Kurt said. "We are very strong, but anything can happen. Players can get hurt, the referee can make mistakes."

"Players can get hurt, yes," the party man said, "but our Mr. Vogel will not make any mistakes. He is what one might call a good referee."

Kurt spun and stared at the man. "But I gave my word."

"Come, come, Major Von Steiner," Lorenz said. "Look behind you. Those are not friendly faces.

We cannot afford to take a chance. We must win." Then he slowly scanned the crowded arena. "From a security point of view, this is all quite mad."

"Yes," Kurt agreed, "quite mad."

With what looked like a mountaineer's pick, the old man tapped at the base of the changing room. He turned, held his finger to his lips, and the men behind him fell silent. The old man pressed his ear to the earth, then nodded and smiled. He had heard the boots of the team as they trampled out of the room on their way to the field.

A blizzard of flowers filled the sky and 50,000 people hooted, whistled, and cheered when Colby, leading the squad, burst out of the stadium's darkness into the arena. A red rose fell into Waldron's lap. He studied it as if it were a strange and foreign object. When the team shouted encouragements, the colonel looked to the pitch and for the first time since "this madness" began, he saw them as people, as players, as soldiers, and he impulsively leapt to his feet and flung the rose out onto the field.

As he ran towards the goal, Hatch raked a handful of flowers off the ground and placed them at the posts. He bowed before the net, and Colby, in a gesture hallowed by superstition, did the captain's job of putting the first practice kick into the empty net.

The players began to lob shots Hatch's way. They ran in short spurts, dribbled, faked tackles, passed. Their spirits rose as the crowd urged them on. Then the Germans entered the field.

Boehm reached for a miniature sound box, twisted a dial, and the broadcast room filled with the sound of thousands cheering. "Now listen to this applause for the German team." He kicked the volume up, then brought it down again. "And why shouldn't they cheer? The boys look splendid."

The team slowed at the sight of the German squad. They were everything Colby said they would be and more. They were Teutonic giants, blond and strong and superb ball handlers. Karl Vogel's whistle blew the Captains to the center of the field. Helmut Rhinegold, looking splendid in his black jersey, ran up to John with his hand extended.

"Good luck, Captain Colby."

"And to you, Rhinegold."

Vogel tossed a coin, John called, and the ball went to the Allies.

Sid Harmer was the first to touch the ball. He brought it down the pitch and passed it to Carlos Rey. The Argentinian danced around two German tacklers, took a fast break, and passed it to Erik Borge.

The squad moved swiftly and easily, the months of practice seen in their strides, in their ability to elude all challenges.

"They look good," Lorenz said to the major.

Kurt was about to answer when the crowd rose to its feet. Pieter van Beck had kicked for a goal and missed by fractions of an inch.

"Very good," Lorenz repeated. "They look very good."

Hatch paced like a lion. The twenty-four foot

mouth of the goal seemed enormous, hungrily inviting the Germans to feed it.

"Let's go!" he shouted. "Let's hustle!"

Boehm was on his feet screaming into the microphone. There was no longer a need for the cheering sound box—the stands beneath his booth trembled with the shouting.

"Germany has the ball . . . Germany is attacking again. This looks dangerous, ladies and gentlemen. They're all over the place!"

A German player dribbled down the wing. Sid Harmer challenged, the German passed inside to a teammate and ran on for the return. Filieu and Clure moved to intercept, but the man in black secured the ball and drove it towards Hatch. He kicked, and the ball, with cannon-shot force, hit the cross bar. Bobby tried to intercept. He leapt and collided with a flying German.

As Bobby fell, Renée clutched the flowers she held so tightly, crushing the stems in her hands. "*Mon Dieu*, Bobby," she said. "*Mon Dieu.*"

The Allies moved the ball up field, the ball going from Fernandez to Terry Brady to Colby. John dribbled hard, looking for a receiver. Pieter broke free of his man and John fired the ball to him. The Dutchman caught the ball with his toe, brought it under control, and was about to shoot it to Filieu when he was tackled hard and late. He hit the ground, and it was minutes before he moved.

Vogel called time out but did not call the foul, and John was on him immediately. "You miserable son of a bitch, a blind man could have seen that foul!"

The Swiss spun on him. "You will not use that

kind of language to me, Captain. I saw no foul, and if you choose to abuse me again, I will put you out of the game."

He then turned and whistled for the stretcher bearers.

John swallowed his fury, spat, and ran towards the crowd that surrounded Pieter. The Dutchman opened his eyes and moaned softly.

Waldron waved a clenched fist. "Foul!" he screamed. "A filthy foul!"

And all around him the outraged French shouted the same.

Kurt shook his head. "Clumsy," he said. "Clumsy and ugly."

Lorenz chose not to hear. He turned to an aide and gave word to alert the security police, then he turned back to the game with a small self-satisfied smile. Vogel was indeed going to be a good referee.

Colby leaned over van Beck: the look of pain in the man's eyes told him that he could be out of the game, that more than just the wind was knocked out of him.

"How are you, Pieter?"

"Bad, the pain it is bad."

Bobby lifted the thin man and placed him on the stretcher.

"That bastard," he growled, then he moved threateningly towards Vogel. "I'm gonna take that prick apart."

John grabbed his blue goalie's jersey and held it tightly. "No you won't. That's exactly what he wants you to do. He'll put you out of the game, and then we'll really be screwed."

John whirled away from him and signaled Milos at the bench. The stubby Czech was still underweight. Not much of his hair had grown back, yet the few months of food and training had restored a bit of bounce to his legs, restored a great deal of his confidence as a man and player. He was smiling broadly as he ran onto the pitch and joined his mates.

Vogel blew the game to life, and the ball was again in motion.

The men sat on the muddy edges of the tunnel and pressed close to a small radio. André punctuated every play with a hard tug of the ear. With two swift passes by his teammates, Rhinegold seized the ball and kicked it hard. The Germans had scored their first goal, and the uncomfortable, restless men were struggling for the ball in their hearts and minds, carrying it down field with drive and determination. They wanted desperately to beat the Boche.

"That was a magnificent play and score by Captain Helmut Rhinegold! Magnificent! And listen to that crowd!"

Boehm's voice filtered through the static, his sound machine almost drowning out his commentary.

"The Germans are attacking again. A pass from Baumann to Manfred Kuntz. This is the smoothest ball passing I have ever seen, ladies and gentlemen. The Nationals seem to be showing contempt for the opposition. The Allies look tired.

The old man wiped a smear of mud from his face.

"Do you think it's all that bad, André?"

"Who knows?" The man shrugged. "I hardly believe the BBC, why should I believe that Nazi bastard?"

André's voice was suddenly lost in the screech of the radio. The Germans had begun a new drive.

John ran the pitch organizing the defense. He yelled and gestured, trying desperately to keep the men on mark. Helmut chested the ball forward and his center back, Schmitt, dribbled it into the penalty area and shot for a goal. Hatch leapt and blocked, but the ball ran loose. In seconds it seemed every man was at the mouth of the goal struggling for the ball, but it was Rhinegold who struck it first. Slowly, painfully, the ball rolled over the line, and the score was two to nothing!

Renée watched the game as if she were running every play. She was exhausted, and sweat gleamed on her brow. She lost track of time but knew that soon, soon those men on the field would be in the bowels of Paris, hopefully on their way to freedom.

Hatch lobbed the ball high into the air and Fernandez trapped it on his chest. The West Indian dropped the ball to his feet and began a dazzling run that brought everyone to his feet. He evaded three tacklers, brought the ball back into the air, caught it on his chest, and juggled it there as he streaked down the pitch. He seemed to be moving to the sound of the stadium, propelled by the 50,000 cheering voices, when Manfred Kuntz, in an illegal charge from the back, brought him down. Two other Germans were instantly over the fallen man; one kicked him in the stomach, the other in the ribs. Incredibly, there was no whistle. Kuntz stole the ball and, to shouts of "shame," brought it past the halfway mark and passed it to Rhinegold who drove it in for a goal.

"Three nil!" Boehm sputtered. "Three nil. Kuntz to Rhinegold, in a magnificently inspired play by the Germans!"

Then he dropped his voice a decible. "Luis Fernandez, the Allied striker, was hurt during the exchange, and the stretcher bearers are carrying him to the changing room. This is a great game, ladies and gentlemen, and the thousands of people who have filled the Colombe Stadium today are witnessing displays of sportsmanship not seen in Paris for many a year."

Again his voice changed. He hit the box and the cheering began. "Now with only a few minutes to go to half time, the Germans attack again!"

Hatch made a brilliant save. He shouted encouragement at the others and cleared the ball away down field, but the Germans cut the missile short and began a relentless drive for another score.

The mouth of the goal was a maze of moving, pushing men, and Hatch strained to see where the ball was. He leapt up and caught a glimpse of it just as Kuntz squared for a kick. Bobby pushed through, grabbed the ball, tossed it free, and was knocked unconscious by the German's boot.

Sid Harmer was the first to see the ball run loose. He side-stepped a tackle, pounded it along the touchline, and began a long dazzling run down the field. He passed to Gunner, who went wide towards the corner flag then laid it square in the path of Harmer, who slashed through for a goal!

Vogel's whistle signaled half time. The score was three to one, and the crowd near hysteria.

CHAPTER SEVENTEEN

With Hatch clinging to his shoulder, Colby burst into the changing room. The American's cheek was swollen into strange proportions, and a dark purple stain began to take hold of the entire right side of his face. Fernandez pulled himself off the bench. He ignored his own pain and walked to Bobby. "Are you all right, man?"

"Yeah, yeah." Bobby tried to grin. "There were these three guys in this alley . . ."

The team pushed behind them. Doug Clure threw his arms around the West Indian and shouted the words every man in the room felt: "We scored! We scored against the bastards!"

The room filled with shouts and the odor of sweat.

"This is a team," Filieu thought. "It sounds like a team, it smells like a team."

"Ice!" someone shouted. "We need ice for our goalkeeper's eye!"

The area filled with the crescendo of excited speech.

"That Swiss son of a bitch—"

"You looked great . . ."

"Watch the Hun striker . . ."

The player's babble built until Colby shouted them down.

"Quiet! God damn it, I said quiet!"

A stillness settled in the room, and the sound of the chipping, clawing picks was heard. A corner section of the floor gave way, and after what seemed like a very long time, a hand poked out of the darkness into the room.

"Barcelona, here I come," Hatch whispered under his breath. He ran to the break in the floor and began to tear at the cracking concrete. "Come on, you guys. Give me a hand here."

The men seemed rooted to the stone.

Completely bewildered, Hatch turned a quizzical face to them. "Hey, let's go! Move your ass. We gotta get the fuck outta here!"

The men began to move forward just as a large chunk of concrete gave way and André pushed through. Bobby grabbed his extended hand, pulled him out of the tunnel, then reached back down for a long ladder.

"*Allez! Vite!* Gentlemen, we go. Quickly, please!"

"You heard the man!" Hatch shouted. "Move!"

But no one did.

Hatch pushed through the men to Pieter. He stopped before the thin man and smiled. "Okay, Dutchman, we're going home."

He lifted him easily into his arms and carried the injured player to the tunnel's mouth.

"Wounded man coming down!" he shouted, and hands reached up and eased Pieter down into the darkness. The walking dead followed silently.

"You're next, Tony. Into the hole."

Tony Morell tucked his broken arm tightly to his side and mounted the first rungs of the ladder. He was about to descend when he looked around at the anxious faces of his teammates.

"If I were in one piece," he said calmly, "I would play. From where I sat, you people looked as if you were just warming up. You looked bloody good." He lifted his good arm and waved. "Ta ta."

"Okay, who's next?" Hatch demanded. The men remained rooted. "Are you guys nuts? Let's go! We ain't got all day. We'll have the assholes banging on the door in a few minutes. Let's go!"

He looked around at their faces. His swollen cheek and half closed eye were beginning to throb.

"I must be losing my mind." His eyes stopped on Luis. "Fernandez, come on. You've got some smarts, get into this hole."

"No, Bobby, I'll wait," the West Indian said. "Let someone else go first. I have some pain, but I can play, I want to play."

"This is crackers," Hatch protested. "Fucking crackers." He rushed to Filieu. "Michel, you voted for this escape. Come on, now."

"No, Bobby," he said, emulating his black colleague. "Let someone else go first."

"All right." There was a touch of desperation

in Bobby's voice. "I'll go first." He waved to André who watched the scene with slackened jaws.

"*Allez!*" Hatch said. "We go!"

"Hold it!" John called. "Just one second."

"We only have one second," Hatch pleaded.

"Then let's use it now." Colby turned to the massed men who stood immobilized before the hole in the floor. "Who wants to go? It's all set, you know. The Resistance is down there, and there are boats that can carry you safely to Spain. Out there," he gestured towards the field, "are a bunch of big Nazis who will possibly kick us all to death. Now make your choice."

The men remained frozen and silent, the seconds passed as if they were minutes, and the minutes hours.

"I'd like to kick in a few teeth myself," Sid Harmer said. "I'm for playing this thing out."

"Me too," Doug agreed. "It's not as if we were being slaughtered, Skipper. We did score a goal."

"*Marche ou Mort!*" Carlos Rey announced. "March or die! That is the motto of the Foreign Legion. I will play!"

"I too," Terry Brady voted, and Erik Borge agreed.

"I'm leaving," Hatch said. "And screw you lunatics." But he didn't move. "Hey, come on, fellas . . ." he pleaded, then he looked into every eye and threw his hands up. "All right, you dumb bastards. If you want to play with a one-eyed goalie who only knows half of what he's doing, then fuck you all. I'll play." He caught Colby's eye and shook his head. "This game'll be the death of me yet. Gimme some ice for this puss of mine and let's play ball!"

On the field, the marching band played "Deutschland Uber Alles" in a vain attempt at drowning out the 50,000 voices singing "La Marseillaise."

The security guards walked the aisles. They eyed each other, checked the safeties on their rifles and automatics, and watched the crowd intently. The situation around them was growing dangerous.

Waldron screamed over the din around him, "Bloody good game, wouldn't you say, Rosey? Pity there won't be more of it. I'll bet our boys . . ." He never finished the statement.

Vogel whistled in the second half, and the teams entered to tumultuous applause.

"God damn that Colby," Waldron muttered through a smile. He knew he would never fully understand the Welshman, but he would never again question his courage.

The sight of the Allies appearing terrified Renée. Something had gone wrong. Were her men dead, captured? Was the Gestapo somehow made aware of the escape? She was on her feet and about to make her way to the aisle, when the old man appeared.

Their commitment to play and the first half's trial by fire tempered the men and made them strong. The desperate anxiety of the first forty-five minutes was gone, and the squad moved in a calm, determined way. They covered retreats, kept in touch with each other with gestures and shouts, and above all, they paced themselves.

The German left winger, Baumann, drove the ball through the center circle. He passed to

Rhinegold, but Carlos Rey intercepted. He back-heeled the ball to Clure, and suddenly the field reversed itself.

The ball went from Clure to Borge to Colby. It all happened so smoothly and quickly that John was left alone with the goalkeeper. He dribbled around him and easily walked the ball into the net.

Von Steiner applauded with the gusto of the connoisseur, but Lorenz was worried. The score was too close, the French in the stands too unruly. He stared silently at the field, his hands nervously clutching his knees.

Boehm understated the beauty of the play. He dulled the roaring of the crowd and forced his voice into something very close to nonchalance: "And so, early in the second half, the Allies have made it three to two. A brave effort against the overwhelming force of the German squad."

Swept along by the gale force of the cheering crowd, the Allies sailed forward. Rhinegold shouted commands, he gestured his men into position. For the first time there was sweat on the golden boy's brow.

Terry Brady trapped a pass from Clure. He changed direction, faked to his right, and the German tacklers lost the precious seconds it took for Terry to head the ball to Milos. The Czechoslovak dribbled towards the goal; he was blinded by sweat, his knee joints screamed with the effort, and he made a desperate kick that rebounded off the bar. In moments the penalty area was a bedlam of hands and flying feet. Rhinegold caught the ball on his toe and back passed it to Kuntz, but Carlos Rey was there. He stole the ball, spun about, and blasted it in for a goal!

The crowd was ranting. Pillows, handkerchiefs, ties, and shirts were waved or flung into the air. A man shouted "victory," and the word, like flame, spread through the stadium.

"Vic—toire! Vic—toire!"

The men of the Resistance ignored the hysteria. They moved from person to person, whispered a message, and the word began its journey through the stadium.

Vogel's whistle was almost inaudible; he waved his arms and shook his head.

"No goal! No goal, ladies and gentlemen," Boehm shouted. "The referee has spotted an infringement, and in a show of some of the worst sportsmanship I've seen in years, is being threatened by the Allied players. Their captain, John Colby, is physically pulling them away."

"Leave the bastard alone!" John bullied. "Get back into position, get back!" He grabbed Sid Harmer's jersey and pulled him away from the frightened Swiss.

"I'll kill him, so help me, I'll kill him!" Sid raved.

"No!" John shouted. "We'll kill him!"

And in the next play, they almost did. Sid dribbled the ball with John as his guard, and Vogel, following the play, ran with them. Harmer passed to Colby, who trapped the ball, quickly changed the direction of his run, and the referee was suddenly trapped between them. John slipped and fell, Vogel toppled with him, and Sid, caught in the triangle, followed them to the ground.

The maneuver was fast, it was perfectly executed, and with the cheers of "victory" ringing in his ears, Vogel was carried from the field with two broken ribs.

"Disgraceful and disgusting," Boehm spat. "Never have I seen such a blatant and unprovoked attack on a referee. Never." He wiped his forearm across his mouth. "Linesman Fisher has taken Vogel's place. There is the whistle. Nine minutes to go, and the score remains Germany three, Allies two. The goal kick is taken, played out to Wedemayer, who finds Kuntz, Kuntz back to Wedemayer, and Germany is on the move."

Wedemayer thought he saw an opening, he feinted to his left, then broke for the right wing. It was a mistake. Fernandez challenged. He dazzled the big man with his footwork and stole the ball. Three Germans were instantly on the defensive. Two tried to tackle, but he bluffed them with a skillfully executed feint that left them momentarily stunned and confused. Then the black man was away with the ball. His flight drew the mass of players to him. Colby called and Luis snapped the ball to him.

The spectators were almost silent as John worked through a maze of defenders. He passed to Brady, Brady to Borge, then back again to John. He could see only a bit of light beyond the wall of charging men. He kicked to Fernandez, and the genius faked a pass and tried a thirty yard chip that flew high over the heads of the charging Germans. The giant blond goalkeeper leapt and the ball grazed his fingertips, hit the inside of the post, and dropped into the net!

It was now three to three and there was madness in the stands. The message of the Resistance had been heard, and the Frenchmen, singly and in small groups, left their seats and slipped into the aisles.

The guards called to each other, called to officers for orders, but the din around them tightly sealed their sound.

The players massed in the penalty area. Manfred Kuntz took a strong shot. He fired the ball into the mouth of the goal, but Hatch, in what seemed like one motion, caught and flung it up field.

Boehm held the microphone tightly in his hands. "Now Helmut Rhinegold is in charge of the ball. He is challenged by Borge but eludes him."

Suddenly the broadcaster shot to his feet. There before him, like a fast moving glacier, the chanting, near hysterical horde of French spectators was slipping out of the stands, pushing everything and everyone in its path towards the pitch.

"*Gott in himmel!*" Boehm exclaimed.

For a moment, Rhinegold forgot that he was on a playing field in the middle of a game. A roaring, hating world was sweeping down on him and his black suited players. A red blur moved by him, and by reflex, the German athlete gave chase.

The Allies were possessed by the madness of the crowd. They drove through the frightened German team with fearful powers. No pass was wrong, no kick could miss, they were in the lap of God.

With only seconds to go, the stadium was delirious. Bobby abandoned the goal and ran with his team. The Allies drove towards the goal. Trinidad to England to Denmark to New York. Bobby screamed as he back-heeled the ball to Colby. John struck hard, the ball hit the bar, ricocheted onto the pitch, and disappeared in the swarm of men.

Now there were no rules or laws of man that could stop this clash of flesh and leather. Struggling for a sight, for a touch of the ball, the players piled on one another with leaps and kicks and flailing arms. A foot pushed the ball out of the ruck. Bobby found it and with a banshee yell drove the ball into the net!

Pandemonium ruled! The trumpets at the creation could not have rivaled the roar that filled Colombe Stadium that day. Strangers became united as brothers and sisters. They became lovers. They hugged and kissed, there were tears and laughter. It was a great reunion of man and his spirit.

The dam of soldiers gave way to the torrent of people, and the French flooded the field. They tore the red uniforms off the sweating men. They gave them civilian clothes and swept them through the stadium out onto the streets of Paris.

The tide of people filled the winding streets and boulevards. It poured into basements and garrets. Then, as if it were an act of God, it ebbed, then disappeared.

EPILOGUE

Bobby looked at himself in the mirror and thought he looked rather snappy in the felt hat, the old brown jacket, and the marvelous pair of torn, oversized trousers someone on the pitch had given him. He was in a safe house somewhere in Montmartre. Children played in the flat below, pigeons roosted and cooed from under the eaves of a house nearby. He smiled at the memory of himself and the team standing naked midfield with ten or fifteen thousand people around them. Then the faces of his friends flashed through his mind. John Colby, a royal pain in the ass, but a great guy whom he loved. Fernandez, the best athlete he had ever known or seen. Pieter, with his broken legs and great courage. He saw them all. Together they had shared a great adventure: they had gambled their lives on an escape to victory and won. Suddenly Bobby was over-whelmed with a great sense of loss and sadness. In his heart of hearts, he knew he would probably never meet any of those magnificent men again.

ABOUT THE AUTHOR

YABO YABLONSKY was born in Brooklyn, New York and attended Brooklyn College and New York University. His screen credits include *Jordi,* which was shown at the Venice Film Festival, and *B. J. Lang Presents,* both of which he wrote and directed. He has also worked extensively throughout Europe. Mr. Yablonsky has owned and operated three theaters as a writer/producer/director and has received four awards for his play writing —two of them from The Ford Foundation and The Rockefeller Foundation. Mr. Yablonsky currently lives in Hollywood, California. His pastimes include sailing the Caribbean. Mr. Yablonsky has been a member of the Actors' Studio in both New York and Los Angeles, and a member of The New Dramatists' Committee in New York.